J VENOKUR ROSS
Venokur, Ross.
The Cookie Company /
WOOD

17 APR 2001

4.4
4.0 pts

the

COOKIE
COMPANY

the COOKIE COMPANY

Ross Venokur

Delacorte Press

Published by
Delacorte Press
an imprint of
Random House Children's Books
a division of Random House, Inc.
1540 Broadway
New York, New York 10036

Visit us on the Web! www.randomhouse.com/kids
Educators and librarians, for a variety of teaching tools, visit us at
www.randomhouse.com/teachers

Library of Congress Cataloging-in-Publication Data
Venokur, Ross.
The Cookie Company / Ross Venokur.
p. cm.
Summary: Thirteen-year-old Alex, the unluckiest boy alive, opens an unusual fortune cookie and is whisked into another world, where he is threatened by the evil game show hostess Cypress Vine.
ISBN 0-385-32680-7
[1. Fortune cookies Fiction. 2. Luck Fiction. 3. Television Fiction. 4. Space and time Fiction.] I. Title.
PZ7.V562Co 2000
[Fic]—dc21   99-35648
                                                                    CIP

The text of this book is set in 14.5-point Bembo.
Book design by Susan Dominguez
Manufactured in the United States of America
February 2000
10 9 8 7 6 5 4 3 2 1
BVG

For
Anna and Sam
and for
Lorayne and Harold
the grandparents

The Cookie Company.

Established 1823.

Once upon a chilly morning
   two centuries ago,
we set up shop in ev'ry town
   and hamlet on the globe,
neither bothering our neighbors
   nor bidding them hello.

And thus we came into this world
   to tap a select few,
to search them out in dire need
   and help them start anew.
I promise, you'll never see us,
   unless we want you to.

There is no story
without a beginning.

prologue

What can I tell you? Every once in a while, and I can't be any more specific than that, a candidate is born. It's my job to make sure each and every one of these candidates ends up here. And that is the way it works. As far as you know.

The trick is to get them here, to help them find this place, to guide them. It's not as complicated as it sounds. You develop a knack for these things when you've been doing them as long as I have—176 years, that's a long time. But don't get too impressed. My job is no different than anyone else's. Really. I punch in, I do the work on my desk, I punch out. I even get one week vacation each year. Not paid, though.

Enough about me. It's time to tell you what you came to hear, the story of the Cookie Company. Well, not *the* story. It's just one of a thousand.

chapter

1

By eight-thirty A.M., Alex Grindlay had already managed to stub his toe, bang his head, drop his toothbrush in the toilet, put in one contact lens and lose the other, sneeze while flossing (sending the dental floss flying up into his head and out his left nostril), slam the closet door on his hair and rip out one of his thick blond curls, tear his shirt, find out firsthand that the step second closest to the bottom of the staircase needed to be repaired, lose his homework, find his homework, burn his toast, burn his homework, discover a cockroach and its ten thousand nearest relatives camping out in his favorite box of cereal, and juice the orange that finally broke the juicer's back (and side and front and other side).

By nine A.M., he had already managed to step in the neighbor's dog's business, trip getting onto the school bus (right in front of Sarah Sachs!), realize that his burnt homework was still sitting by the front door (where he put it so that he couldn't possibly forget it), act as the target for a nauseous pigeon at the exact moment a stray Frisbee bounced off his head, get stuck in his locker, wander into the girls' (as opposed to the boys') bathroom, and get stuck in his locker, again.

All in all, it was shaping up to be a typical day for Alex.

His teacher, Ms. Figelman, had just finished taking roll call when Alex finally broke out of his locker and stumbled into class. Ms. Figelman was one of those shortish, stoutish, frumpyish, dis-combobulatedish, peculiarish teachers. Instead of walking, she waddled like a penguin, causing her giant head of brown hair to flop this way and that way and over and back.

Ms. Figelman had the kind of hair that swallowed things up. Whenever she scratched her head, a pencil would fall out, or a stick of chewing gum, or half a chicken sandwich. One time, the remote control from her television popped out. "Well, what do you know?" she yipped. "I've been looking all over for this!"

Despite her appearance, however, when Ms. Figelman spoke, the class paid complete attention. Truth to tell, it had little to do with what she said. It was how she said it. When Ms. Figelman spoke, she spit—a lot. Everyone knew you had to pay attention to the teacher to avoid her sprinklers, or you'd risk a soaking.

After marking Alex present, she put the attendance book away and turned to address her class. "For those of you who may not know," she began as the entire first row bobbed to its left and narrowly avoided the sudden showers, "today is Alex's birthday. Therefore, before presenting our essays on the Wonderful World of Warts, Fungi, and Other Things That Grow on Our Feet, I think we should sing 'Happy Birthday.' "

Ms. Figelman, who took things like singing extremely seriously, warmed up her voice with a rapid series of *Mi mi mi mi mi mi mi*'s. The entire class took cover. Well, the entire class save Alex. He was too amazed.

"Someone remembered my birthday?" he asked himself. It was the first time in his life that someone had remembered. And today of all days, when bad luck should be around more than ever before.

"It's not every day that the unluckiest boy in the world turns the unluckiest number in the world—thirteen," Alex thought. A wad of Ms. Figelman's saliva smacked into his forehead.

"Now remember, class," Ms. Figelman insisted, "e-nun-ci-ate, and diphthong!"

The students just sort of looked at each other. Someone tapped Alex on the shoulder. It was the girl in the seat behind him, Sarah Sachs. As far as Alex was concerned, no one had ever made braided pigtails look so good.

"Diphthong?" she giggled.

Alex shrugged.

"And a-one," Ms. Figelman began, "and a-two, and a-three, 'Happy—' "

RING! The fire alarm went off.

"All right, everyone," Ms. Figelman slobbered, "leave your seats and proceed to the nearest exit in an orderly manner."

By the time the class was seated again, after

forty-five minutes of standing outside waiting for the drill to end, Ms. Figelman had forgotten all about Alex's birthday. She only had one thing on her mind: the Wonderful World of Warts, Fungi, and Other Things That Grow on Our Feet.

"Oh well," Alex mumbled, and he started to think up excuses for why he didn't have his homework. The truth about burning it in the toaster and leaving it by the front door was too unlikely. Ms. Figelman would never buy it.

There was another tap on his shoulder. Once again the exquisite Sarah Sachs. "Happy birthday," she whispered. Then she smiled. Alex could see his reflection in her shiny silver braces. He felt the same way about her smile as he did about her pigtails. No one had ever looked so good in braces, and, for a brief moment, he considered writing a thank-you card to Sarah's orthodontist.

That was the last time anybody broached the subject of Alex's birthday. There was one promising moment later that afternoon, though, when Ms. Figelman suddenly perked up in the middle of a tedious lecture on why a peanut is actually a vegetable and not a nut, and she screeched, "Oh, oh, oh, oh, oh, oh, oh, oh! I almost forgot!" She looked right at Alex, smiled big, and said, "Pop quiz!"

And that was all Alex got for his thirteenth birthday. One pop quiz.

Eventually, three o'clock rolled around and everyone made a break for it. Two steps into his run for freedom, Alex's brand-spanking-new knapsack fell apart at the seams—really, the thread just unraveled—and everything inside dumped out all over the floor. By the time he finished tracking down his last pencil, the halls of Fox Meadow were completely empty. He made it outside just in time to see the school bus drive off.

"Oh well," he mumbled, and he started to walk home.

"Hey, Alex!" someone hollered. He turned around and was blinded by the sunlight bouncing off the sparkling silver that decorated Sarah Sachs's perfectly crooked teeth. "Wait up!" she called, and skipped over.

"Miss the bus?" she asked.

"Yep." Alex nodded. "I pretty much miss it every day. What about you?"

"I was on it, but then I remembered that I left

my violin in my locker. So I had to go back. Do you know you're wearing two different shoes?"

Alex looked down. She was right. He was wearing one white sneaker and one polished brown penny loafer (complete with a government misprinted two-headed penny tucked into it).

"Oh well," he said.

"So," Sarah asked, "you want to walk home together?"

"No!"

Sarah's smile disappeared, as did her braces.

"I mean," Alex explained, "yes, I do. It's just, I don't think it's a good idea."

"Why not?" Sarah asked, a bit offended.

"Because . . ." Alex took a deep breath, let it out, and admitted, "I'm the unluckiest boy in the world, and I don't want you to catch what I have."

"What do you have?" Sarah asked.

"*Hoodooitis.*"

"Hoodooitis? That's not a disease. I don't even think it's a word!"

"Yes, it is," Alex insisted.

"Okay, then what does it mean?"

"It means that I have a swollen *Hoodoo*."

"What's a Hoodoo?"

"The Hoodoo is the place where all bad luck comes from."

Sarah just looked at him.

"Really," Alex insisted. "We all have one. Even you."

"I do not have a Hoodoo!" Sarah firmly stated, offended all over again.

"Of course you do. Have you ever had something bad happen to you for no reason?"

"Well, yes," she had to admit. "One time I blew a bubble so big with my grape bubble gum that I couldn't see where I was going and I walked right into a wall. I had grape bubble gum stuck to my face for hours, and when my mom finally got it off, I had a big black-and-blue welt on my forehead that didn't go away for a week."

"See!" Alex said. "You have a Hoodoo, and sometimes it swells up and bad things like that happen."

"Come on," Sarah said, still not buying it.

"When it happened, did you feel a pain in your stomach, even though you hit your head?"

"Um, yeah, I think I did."

"That's how you know your Hoodoo is swollen. You feel a pain in your stomach. Or sometimes just a tingle. It's no big deal," Alex explained. "It's like any other *itis*—tonsillitis, appendicitis, fingeritis, noseitis—after a while, the Hoodoo goes back to its usual size and the bad-luck streak ends. That's when the pain goes away. At least that's how it works for most people."

"But not for you?" Sarah guessed.

"Nope. I have a chronic case of Hoodooitis. One hundred percent, completely incurable."

"You've been to a doctor about it?"

"Um, no."

"Then how do you know Hoodooitis even exists?"

"I just do." Alex shrugged.

"Well . . ." Sarah smiled. "It doesn't sound like it's too catchy. I'll take my chances. Let's go." And she started to walk.

"Just don't say I didn't warn you," Alex said, and he quickly caught up to her.

With two exceptions, the walk home was relatively uneventful. Exception one jumped over a fence in the form of a dog who decided Alex's shirt looked like a great snack.

"Oh well." Alex shrugged as the dog ran off with his delicious T-shirt.

"Aren't you going to go after it?" Sarah asked.

"What's the point?" Alex responded. "It's my Hoodooitis again."

And wouldn't you know, when exception two drove by in the form of a bus splashing through a puddle, Alex just stood there as the wave soaked him to the bone. When Sarah, who'd had the sense to step back and avoid the drencher, pointed out that Alex should have moved out of the way, all he could say was, "Oh well."

Outwardly, Alex and his "Oh wells" seemed to be rolling with the punches. But by the time he reached Sarah Sachs's house (shirtless and dripping), he wished he were dead.

"I see what you mean about your Hoodooitis," Sarah offered awkwardly. "You have terrible luck. Do you want to come in and dry off or something?"

"No thanks," Alex replied.

"Well . . ." Sarah smiled uncomfortably. "I'll see you at school tomorrow." She walked up the path and disappeared into her house. Alex continued on his way home.

A moment later he heard Sarah yell, "Hey, Alex!" He spun around and saw her head sticking out of her bedroom window. "I bet you a piece of pizza and a Coke that there is a cure for your disease!" As she pulled her head back inside the window, a ray of sun bounced off her braces and landed in Alex's left eye, blinding him. He stumbled backward, tripped, and knocked himself out on a suspiciously low tree branch.

He came to a few minutes later, picked himself up, brushed himself off, and headed for home— all the while reassuring himself with a mouthful of "Oh wells."

chapter

When Alex got home, wet, shirtless, and headachy, his dad was busy watching TV. That was all his dad ever did. In fact, Alex's thirteenth birthday doubled as the thirteenth anniversary of the day Alex's dad sat down in his recliner, kicked up his feet, and turned on the Game Show Station. His dad had not stood up since. Really.

"Hey, Dad!" Alex yelled as he slammed the front door. He marched upstairs, slipped into a new shirt, crossed the tiny hallway, and flipped on the lights in his father's bedroom. "How was your day?"

"Great!" Alex's dad answered. "You will never guess what happened today."

"Hmmm." Alex pretended to think it over. "Let me see. Did someone win something on some show?"

"Exactly!" Mr. Grindlay nodded, as excited as could be. "Pamela—she's a newlywed from central Kansas—spun for an eighteen-foot yacht on *The Deal Wheel*. And guess what?"

"What?"

"She got it!"

"What's a woman going to do with a boat in the middle of Kansas?" Alex asked.

"Who cares?" Mr. G. sighed. "She won! What luck. Imagine that."

The annoyingly peppy theme music of *The Puzzle Pyramid* filled the room, and Alex's dad whipped around to face the TV. "*The Puzzle Pyramid* is my absolute favorite game show." He smiled. The truth was, Mr. G. said that about every game show.

Alex knew there was no point in talking to his dad now that the show was on. The trick was to catch him during the commercials. Instead of going off to do his homework as he usually did, he sat down in front of the TV. There wasn't *much* chance his dad would remember Alex's birthday, but maybe if they sat there long enough, he might.

Mr. G. stared at the TV, mesmerized by the host of *The Puzzle Pyramid,* a strikingly elegant woman named C. C. deVine. She was bone thin and had wispy red hair that shot out in all directions. Her long neck disappeared into her deep green dress. She had a perfect nose, a sculpted chin, and jet-black eyes. The whole eyeball. No white, no color, all black. The perfect contrast to her blindingly white teeth.

"That woman freaks me out," Alex said.

"C. C. deVine? She's the most beautiful woman in the world," Mr. Grindlay insisted in a dreamy way. "See how she looks at me?"

Alex shook his head. "I guess I'd better go do my homework."

Ms. Figelman had given the class a tough assignment. They had to create their own board games. She said it would teach them problem solving, chance, and creative thinking. Alex thought she was crazy, but hey, she was the teacher.

Alex dug through the basement until he found

exactly what he didn't know he was looking for. A triangular piece of Plexiglas that used to be the top of an ugly table.

"Cool," Alex thought. He had played a kajillion games in his lifetime, but he'd never seen a triangular game board, or a clear one for that matter.

Back in his room, Alex used a black pen to divide the triangle into forty-five smaller triangular spaces. He colored six of them green with a Magic Marker. In each of the board's three corners he wrote START HERE. Then he stuck a toothpick into a pink eraser that he had yanked off the end of a pencil and glued the eraser to the center of the board. Once the glue was dry, he stapled a small yellow triangular piece of paper, with the word WINNER written on it, to the top of the toothpick. It looked just like a small flag. Alex was satisfied with his work. Then he made two special dice out of Styrofoam, and wrote out cards with different options.

Now that he had a board and pieces, he needed rules. So he got busy writing some down.

Twist of Fate
Rules by Alex Grindlay

1. Whoever gets to the WINNER space first wins.
2. Each of the 3 players starts in a START HERE space.
3. Player 1 rolls the first die. (The one with the numbers on it. There are two number 1's, two number 2's, and two number 3's.)
4. Player 1 can (a) either move the number thrown on the die, or (b) chance it and roll the second die (the one with the words written on it).
5. Two sides of the second die read DOUBLE FORWARD, two sides read EVEN STEVEN, and two sides read DOUBLE BACKWARD. If player 1 rolls:
   (a) DOUBLE FORWARD, player 1 moves twice the original roll.
   (b) EVEN STEVEN, player 1 moves the original roll.
   (c) DOUBLE BACKWARD, player 1 moves

twice the original roll *away from*
the WINNER space.

6. Player 2 and player 3 do the same as
player 1.

7. If any player lands on a green triangle—a
Twist of Fate space—that player selects a
Twist of Fate card. Before the card is
read, the player chooses option A or B.
(Every card has two options: A and B.
One is Good Luck and one is Bad Luck.)
The player follows the card's directions.

By the time Alex had finished writing the rules,
it was seven o'clock. His stomach had been rum-
bling for the last hour. His dad was always too
busy watching the Game Show Station to remember to be hungry, so Alex always took care of
dinner. Otherwise, they would never have eaten.
Alex put the game into a box and wandered back
into his father's bedroom, phone book in hand.

Mr. G. was teetering on the edge of his seat,
completely captivated by a man in tight-fitting
orange-and-blue-plaid pants and a short-sleeved
button-down shirt that didn't quite cover his

belly. The peculiar fellow was doing his best to make it through the Lightning Round on *The Crazy Clue Course Challenge*—one of those silly physical game shows. Unfortunately, when the plaid contestant slid down the oversized drinking straw into the humongous ice cream float, he completely abandoned any attempt to get through the course in less than sixty seconds as he was supposed to, and tried, instead, to drink the entire two-story-high float. By the time the sixty-second buzzer rang, the contestant had sunk his head so deeply inside the forty-pound scoop of chocolate ice cream, he could hear neither the buzzer nor the sound of his wife pounding on the side of the glass. "Harold!" she shouted. "No! You're making an embarrassment of yourself! Harold! Harold!"

"Real shame," Dad muttered under his breath, and he sank back into his recliner. He instantly perked up again, however, when the camera focused on the show's host, an elegant woman with wispy red hair and a deep green dress. "Thanks for watching *The Crazy Clue Course Challenge*," the host said. "My name's Cy P. Vine, and I'll see *you* again tomorrow."

As the show cut to a commercial, Cy P. Vine flashed a brilliant white smile, and Mr. Grindlay yelped, "Did you see that? She smiled at me. Did you see?"

"I saw," Alex told his dad, knowing better than to argue.

"So, what's that you got there?" his dad asked.

"Phone book. It's time to order dinner. What should we have?"

Before his dad could answer, the doorbell rang.

"Don't bother getting up," Alex said to himself, since his dad had already been recaptivated by the next game show, *The Nice Price,* and its lovely host, C. P. Veene. Alex bounced down the steps to answer the door.

"Who is it?" Alex demanded through the closed front door.

"Chinese delivery," a peppy voice replied.

"We didn't order any Chinese food."

"Is this nine Park Road?"

"Yes."

"Then this is your Chinese food."

Alex peeked through the window. An old Chinese man in a purple tweed cap stood outside. He held a white plastic bag with a brown paper bag stuffed with red-and-white cartons of Chinese food sticking out of it.

The deliveryman had incredibly bushy eyebrows. He wore a purple tweed jacket with the name SAL stitched over its breast pocket. His shorts matched his jacket and cap. His green socks were pulled knee-high and disappeared into purple shoes with big gold buckles.

He waved to Alex through the window and flashed a large, inviting smile. He looked old, but he moved fast. He took off his cap, twirled it across the length of his arm, and said, "Express Delivery!" He flipped his hat up into the air, and it landed snugly on his head.

"Very express," Alex said. "I didn't even order yet. Actually, we didn't even decide on Chinese yet. I think you've got the wrong address."

"Your name is Alex Grindlay?" the old deliveryman asked.

"How do you know that?" Alex demanded.

"And is today your birthday?"

"Yes," Alex admitted.

The old-timer looked up at Alex's house. "Redbrick house, white shutters, arched doorway, broken chimney. Like I said, this is your Chinese food."

"Well, hold on a minute," Alex said, still a bit skeptical. "I have to go upstairs and get some money from my dad."

"No charge," the old Chinese man said with another huge smile. "Birthday present." And he placed the bag of food on Alex's doormat. Then he turned around, hopped into the air, clicked his heels together, skipped down the path, and climbed into the most peculiar car Alex had ever seen. It was bubbly and blue and green and purple, and taller than it was long. Plus, it had five wheels. The man whizzed up a ladder and climbed into the car through its roof. He honked the horn, which sounded more like a burping pigeon than a honk, saluted Alex, and drove off. The extremely large rear license plate read EXPRESS DELIVERY.

What a strange surprise. Was it possible that Alex's dad had remembered his birthday after all? "How weird," Alex said, though there was no one around to hear him.

Alex took a deep breath, and his head filled with the wonderfully nauseating scent of moo-shu pork, shrimp in lobster sauce, General Chow's chicken, vegetable egg rolls, panfried dumplings, barbecued spareribs, veggie lo mein, white rice, and green tea. His stomach grumbled *Feed me!* and he bolted back upstairs.

There was a commercial on, so Mr. G. heard Alex come in and smelled the pungent birthday feast.

"That was quick," he remarked.

"Express Delivery," Alex explained. He handed his dad a carton of noodles and a pair of chopsticks. Since Mr. Grindlay never left his chair and Alex hated doing dishes, they ate every meal directly out of whatever container it was delivered in.

Approximately two commercial breaks later, after Alex and his dad had gorged themselves on the delicious food, Alex began rummaging around for the fortune cookies. He probed the cartons that were strewn all over the floor, flipped over bags of tea, tossed aside soy sauce and hot mustard packets alike, and searched both the plastic and the paper bag. But there were no fortune cookies.

"Oh well," he told himself, and he leaned back to watch some more TV with his dad. Two solid hours of game shows—all hosted by long-necked, red-haired, black-eyed women in elegant green dresses—was all Alex could handle. He finally kissed his dad good night, brushed his teeth, and slid into some pj's. For a brief moment he considered calling Sarah Sachs to say good night, but decided that, given his Hoodooitis, that would only be a catastrophe.

As he lay in bed staring at the ceiling, Alex thought how much nicer his birthday could have been if only he'd had a mom. But that was part of the deal of being the unluckiest boy in the world. No mom.

chapter

A gaggle of drunken Ogres sat around an enormous banquet table and feasted. From the dark corner of the dining hall, Alex watched the colossal creatures. He was having his nightmare again. "Oh well," he dreamed.

Comparatively no bigger than a mouse, Alex stared up at the hairy, mean, dirty giants. When he breathed in, the stench almost knocked him out. "It smells like three-day-old garbage," he thought. He tucked his nose into the collar of his pajama top and watched. Some of the Ogres had one eye. Others had two, three, or even four. They all had the same enormous yellow-and-brown, mold-covered, jagged teeth—finely crafted tools, but for what diet?

One Ogre belched, and a bone popped out of his mouth. He reached into the large bowl in the center of the table, searched around, and discovered there was no food left.

"Enough!" screamed the Ogre. The massive creature stood up. He was extra huge, extra hairy, and extra dirty. He wore a tarnished crown.

"Eww." Alex shuddered as he caught a whiff of the king. "He smells like *eight*-day-old garbage. Maybe that's why they made him king."

"Ogres," the king growled, "we have feasted for ninety-seven days straight!"

The Ogres belched with joy and cheered, "Hooray for King Odorf!"

"Ogres, you do not understand." Odorf shook his head. "Our supplies have run out."

"No!" objected a one-eyed Ogre. "That cannot be!"

"Yes," barked Odorf, "it is so, Og." A tear formed in Og's one eye. "The fridge is empty," King Odorf continued. "There are no more Kechish elves left for us to devour."

"Elves?" Alex said to himself. "Poor guys."

"Now what?" Odorf asked. "We can't live on artificial-butter-flavored elf topping alone, can we?"

"No!" roared his dirty countrymen.

"We are Ogres," Odorf proudly stated. "We deserve better. At sunrise, we raid Kechland again!"

The Ogres hollered, and Alex had to cover his tiny ears for fear that they might burst.

The Ogres' cheers grew louder, and Alex dreamed himself sitting in a tree, in the center of a ring of jagged, slate-black mountains. By the light of the rising sun, he was able to see the army of Ogres bounding down the mountains of Ogremany into the helpless valley of Kechland.

The tiny Kechish elves were no match for the ferocious and hungry Ogres. One by one, the beasts plucked up the elves and tossed them into massive potato sacks that they wore slung over their backs. They stepped on houses. They ransacked bowling alleys. And they captured every single Kechish elf.

Alex now dreamed himself on top of Odorf's

sack. He peered inside. The king had caught at least a hundred elves, and as he bounded back to Ogremany, Alex watched the prisoners argue about what to do.

"There's still much ground to cover between here and Ogremany," the queen of Kechland suggested. "We can cut a hole in the sack, unravel some of the material to use as a rope, and escape." Many of her companions nodded in agreement. But her own husband, the Kechish king, was not willing to fight.

"What's the point?" he asked. "If we escape, it will only upset the Ogres more."

Many of the Kechish elves nodded and grumbled. "The king's right. We don't want to anger the Ogres."

"Anger the Ogres!" the queen screamed in disbelief. "Who cares? We have to try to escape. We can't give up, we have to fight!"

"Yes!" screamed the Kechish citizens who sided with the queen. "We will fight!"

"What's the point?" the king asked his beautiful wife again. "We're going to be beaten no matter what we do."

"Why?" the queen argued. "Why will we be beaten?"

"Because," the king explained, "we are Kechish, and the Ogres are much bigger. In the end, all Kechish get devoured by Ogres. It is our lot."

"So?" asked the queen.

"So?" answered the king. "What's the point?"

Alex woke up before the queen could answer, just as he always did. His dad's TV was blaring, so he pulled himself out of bed and trudged down the hallway to turn it off.

Mr. Grindlay was fast asleep. A strand of drool dangled out of the corner of his mouth and moved up and down as he breathed in and out. Still half-asleep himself, Alex crossed the room to shut off the television.

CRUNCH!

"Uh-oh." Alex glanced down to see what he had stepped on. A fortune cookie. Four fortune cookies, actually. (Well, three, if you didn't count the one Alex had just obliterated.)

"Where did you come from?" Alex mumbled. "You weren't here before. I looked." He plopped down onto the ground, rubbed his eyes to be sure

they were open, and sifted through the annihi-
lated cookie's crumby mess. He raised the
cookie's paper fortune into the television's bluish
light.

THE COOKIE COMPANY.

ESTABLISHED 1823.

"That's not a fortune," Alex grumbled. He
flipped the small scrap of white paper over to see
what was written on the other side. Nothing.

"It's just a stupid ad," Alex groggily com-
plained as he cracked open the second cookie.
"Maybe you'll have something more fortunate to
say."

GO THERE.

"Huh?" Alex figured that either he was stupid
or the cookies were stupid, because the fortunes
didn't make sense.

" 'Go there' isn't a fortune, either. Then
again," he said, considering, "what if 'there' is
some really cool place? Well, it doesn't matter. I

don't have any idea where there is. I couldn't possibly go without an address. So how about you?" he asked the third cookie. "What do you have to say for yourself?"

1228 GEISEL LANE.

"Weird!" A tingle ran up Alex's spinal cord, hit his brain, turned around, retreated down his back, zipped into his leg, and didn't stop until it hit the nail on his big toe. Alex shuddered. Geisel Lane was in his town—way off to the other side, but still, that was a huge coincidence. Wasn't it?

"Why should I go *there*?" he asked the fourth and final cookie. "What's there for me?"

YOUR FORTUNE.

"Give me a break!" Alex laughed.

He popped up to turn off the TV and go back to sleep. As he reached for the Power button, he was overcome with the eeriest sensation. A face filled the screen. A skeletally thin woman with red wispy hair, pure black eyes, and brilliant white teeth. She wasn't talking. She wasn't moving. She was just staring straight ahead. As crazy as it sounded, Alex felt that she was watching him. As he pressed the Power button with his index finger, their eyes met. Then she was gone.

Alex turned around and headed for bed. But once again his foot knocked into something on the floor. A fifth fortune cookie.

"Where did *you* come from?" he demanded of the treat as he picked it up. He was half inclined to just throw the thing away. But curiosity overcame him. So he cracked it open. Before he could even blink, Alex disappeared.

chapter

Alex, dressed in his school clothes again, gripped the rusted-out bars of the beat-up gate that surrounded the enormous factory building that sat on lot 1228 Geisel Lane. He looked up and down the dark street. "How have I never noticed this place before?" he wondered. "And where are my pajamas?"

The brick building was massive and creepy. Half the windows were boarded up with rotten wood. The other half had been smashed in. A large section of the roof was simply not there anymore.

"This is my fortune?" Alex thought. "It gives

me the heebie-jeebies." But since he had been dragged this far, he pushed the rusty wrought-iron gate. It creaked open, fighting Alex every step of the way until finally it gave up and fell right off its hinges, crashing to the ground with a deafening clamor.

The noise spooked Alex. He almost decided to go home. But something on the face of the decrepit factory building caught his eye. He approached the building. The bright red door looked brand-new. Alex could see his reflection in the rich, shiny, fresh red paint. It had a sparkling gold doorknob and equally sparkling hinges. In the middle of the door there was a matching gold plaque with black engraved letters.

THE COOKIE COMPANY.
ESTABLISHED 1823.

"I guess this is it," he thought. He took a deep breath, pushed the door open, and walked inside.

"Helloooo," he half shouted. "Anybody home?" There was no answer.

He passed through what had probably once been a reception area, through another series of doors, and into a long corridor. He wandered down the dark hallway and flicked switches up and down. "I wonder if Sarah Sachs will believe me when I tell her I explored the old, abandoned factory that nobody ever knew was there."

At the end of the hallway, Alex passed through another door. It opened onto a factory floor. Though this room was as dismal and decrepit as the rest of the building, a gigantic contraption took up the entire space. It gleamed as if it had been polished only moments before.

The shiny silver monster was made up of levers and buttons and springs and lights and pumps and accordions and tubes and pipes and twists and turns and coils and slats and boxes and balls, and one long purple conveyor belt, which stuck out like a tongue that had spent the day licking a grape lollipop.

"Beauty, isn't she?"

Alex jumped at the sound of the strange voice and swung around. There he was, face-to-face with a small old Chinese man in a purple tweed cap that perfectly matched his jacket and shorts. The Express Delivery man.

"Name's Salvador," the man explained as he grabbed Alex's hand and shook it. "Most folks call me Sal." Alex didn't respond. He was fixated on a single silver hair growing out of Sal's wrinkled cheek. The hair had grown past Sal's chin, past his shoulders, past his waist, all the way to his knees. Alex wondered why he hadn't noticed it when Sal delivered dinner.

"So," the old man chirped, "I see you got my invitation."

"The c–c–cookies?" Alex stammered, completely overwhelmed by—well, by everything.

Sal nodded. He opened his arms wide and proclaimed, "Welcome to the Cookie Company!"

"Th–Thank you," Alex stammered, completely amazed. "Um, why am I here?"

"Why are you here?" Sal laughed. "Why are you here? Why, you're here for your birthday present, my boy."

"My birthday present?" Alex said. "But you already gave me all that food."

"Well, I couldn't send you off on an empty stomach, could I?"

"Send me off? Where am I going?"

"In due time." Sal waved a finger in Alex's

37

face. "In due time. For now, take a look at this." Sal pushed a large red button on the side of the machine.

BOIING!

A five-foot-long silver lever popped out of a small crevice. There was a noise, like the sound of an army of tiny people blowing up balloons.

Huff after huff.

Puff after puff.

Alex looked around, but he couldn't tell where the noise was coming from.

Then, POP!

A red ball emerged from the end of the silver lever.

"Why don't you do the honors?" Sal asked Alex.

"Me?" Alex was flattered, though he wasn't really sure why.

Sal nodded. "Yes, you."

Alex grabbed the red handle and yanked the silver lever down. All at once the lights on the machine lit up (the red ones lit red, the blue ones lit blue, the green ones lit green, the yellow ones lit yellow, the speckled ones lit speckled, and the striped ones lit striped), and all the springs sprang, and the twists twisted, and the turns turned, and the pumps pumped, and the tubes tubed, and the coils coiled, and the buttons buttoned (and un-buttoned), and the pipes piped, and the accordi-ons accordioned, and the boxes boxed, and the balls balled, and the slats slatted.

All the while, there were WHIZZES!
and POPS!
and BANGS!
and BELCHES!
and SNEEZES!
and SPLURTS!
and GURTS!
and SPLATS!
and BOIINGS!
and DINGS!
and WHOPS!
and ZINGS!

An awful grinding filled the room. Rainbow-colored smoke shot out of every opening in the machine. The grape-lollipop-licker-looking con-veyor belt started to move. There was something on it, coming Alex's way.

Alex took a step to the left to get out of the way, but the purple conveyor belt followed him. So Alex took two steps back, and the purple belt grew two steps longer. It seemed determined to deliver its package to him. Sal saw that the boy was missing the point, so he picked up the small parcel himself. The machine made a loud SSSPPPLLLLLLLL! of a noise and shut off.

"For you," Sal said, and he handed Alex a brown leather satchel. Alex untied the drawstrings, excited to see what fabulous thing all those noises, lights, buzzers, tubes, and pumps had made him.

He was disappointed.

"Fortune cookies?" Alex mumbled. "Oh well."

"This is a fortune cookie company, you'll recall," Sal reminded the disappointed boy. "You were hoping for something more exciting, perhaps?"

Alex shrugged. "Well, it's just that I already had five cookies at home. And now it's almost midnight, and I don't know how on earth I got here—or how I'll ever get home—and all I have to show for this is five more cookies."

"They're not just *any* fortune cookies, Alex."

Sal waved his finger in the boy's face again. "They're *your* fortune cookies."

"I don't understand."

"You don't need to." Sal smiled. "I've been in this business for a long time. A hundred seventy-six years, to be exact."

Alex shook his head. "No way!"

"Why not?"

"Because nobody lives that long?"

"And why not?" Sal challenged. "Because you've never met anyone that old?"

"Well," Alex admitted, "yes."

"But it's true, my boy. I am a hundred ninety-six years old."

"Hold on." Alex had him now. "You just said you were a hundred seventy-six years old."

"Wrong," Sal corrected him. "I said I've been in this business for a hundred seventy-six years. What do you think, that I started working the day I was born? That would be ridiculous."

"It *is* ridiculous," Alex thought. "*All* of this is ridiculous."

"It's time to start changing the way you look at things, my boy."

"Why?"

"Because you're missing out. You look at everything straight on, Alex. And see only bad things happening. You have to find a way to see things backward, and sideward, and crossward, and flippedward, and upsidedownward, and mixedupward and insideoutward. Otherwise, my boy, you may never change."

"So?" Alex asked.

"So, do you know what happened to the boy who never changed?"

Alex shrugged. "What?"

"He stayed the same," Sal explained. "You don't want that, do you?"

"It doesn't matter what I want, Sal," Alex told the strange factory worker. "I have no control over what happens. Everything that can go wrong, does. I have Hoodooitis, and that's that."

"Oh, right," Sal agreed. "The Hoodooitis. Like I said, Alex, you have to learn to examine things differently. In the meantime, would you like to know what I've figured out about Hoodooitis over the past hundred ninety-six years?"

"Sure," Alex answered, surprised to meet an

adult who acknowledged the existence of his disease.

"Sometimes it's best to ignore it and to dive right in."

"Dive right into what?" Alex wasn't entirely sure he wanted to know the answer.

"You'll figure it out," Sal assured Alex in his whistly voice. "Have some faith in yourself." Sal then patted Alex on the back and added, "I think it's time."

"Time for what?" Alex was still completely baffled.

"For you to have a cookie."

"Yeah?" Alex asked in a confused way.

"Yeah," Sal assured him in a not-so-confused way.

Alex peered into the sack of cookies. "Which one?"

"Doesn't really matter."

So Alex picked one at random.

"That looks like a good one." Sal smiled. Alex flipped it around in his hand and stared at it for a moment. Then he looked back up at Sal, who nodded him on with another encouraging smile.

"Oh well, here goes nothing."

As Alex cracked open the first cookie, he swore he heard Sal say, "I'll see you on the other side." But there was no telling for sure, because the moment Alex snapped that fortune cookie in half, he disappeared.

**Don't be hasty;
nothing is as it seems.**

chapter

Sal was gone. The machine was gone. The entire factory was gone. You think *you're* confused—just imagine how Alex felt as he traveled down a moving sidewalk, through what he could only guess was another dimension. There were other moving sidewalks just like the one Alex was on—above, below, and parallel to Alex's, moving in all directions. There were even a few running vertically.

Alex was scared and interested and confused and even a little sweaty. There were no boundaries to this place. And there was no particular color either. That is to say, the color was constantly changing. First green, then red, then violet, then yellow, then orange, then peach.

At first Alex was so shocked by his sudden teleportation that he stopped breathing. Then he was the one changing colors—to an interesting bluish shade. Fortunately, just before he passed out, he gasped for air.

The oxygen hit his brain and Alex's senses really kicked in. There was music playing, and he recognized the song. It was one of his favorites, and it was playing at what he considered the perfect volume. He also recognized the smell of this place. It smelled like Sarah Sachs sitting behind him in class. Apple-blossom shampoo.

"Where am I?" Alex whispered out loud, just because it seemed like the kind of place where a person should whisper. He moved several more feet down the sidewalk. "What am I supposed to do now?"

Neon-green letters appeared in the thin air above his head. They spelled out ALEX GRINDLAY. Next to the name, a blinking arrow pointed to the left of the sidewalk. The piece of the sidewalk that Alex was standing on forked off in that direction, while somehow the rest of the sidewalk just kept moving straight.

"Amazing!" Alex whispered. He moved forward, and though he could see nothing around him, he felt as if he were being pushed through a wall of Jell-O. Then there was an awesome flash of light.

Alex stood alone in a sprawling green field, his sack of fortune cookies still in his hand.

He felt a pain in his stomach. His Hoodooitis was acting up. He still had no idea where he was. This field didn't exist—according to any map known to man, that is.

It sort of looked like George Field, the park where he played his Little League games, Alex thought. He had broken a different bone every season since he'd started playing baseball six years earlier, but he loved the game anyway. Only this field didn't have a fence and it didn't seem to end. And it was much greener.

Somewhere between feeling scared and nervous, and between being confused and curious, Alex remembered the fortune cookie. "Well," he asked the opened cookie, "what do you have to say about all this?"

DON'T BE HASTY;

NOTHING IS AS IT SEEMS.

"Typical. My magic fortune, made especially for me by that crazy machine, is a big, boring nothing. Thanks a lot, Sal," he said to his misfortune cookie. "How am I supposed to get out of here?"

He took a step forward, and SPLASH!

The field disintegrated around him. Alex had fallen up to his neck into a massive ocean. He had to tread water as quickly as possible to keep from drowning.

He looked around frantically, but there was no sign of the field. All he could see was water. He was floating in a vast sea, and from the look of things, he was going to be there for a long, long, long, long, long time.

"Oh well," he told himself. But this time, in this place, his "Oh wells" were powerless. Their balmlike, soothing effect, which had always allowed Alex to dismiss any unfortunate event, was useless here. Floating in an ocean by himself simply was not a situation covered by the protective "Oh well" umbrella. Poor Alex. If someone hadn't rowed up at that exact moment, he probably would have lost it. But someone did row up, in a tiny rubber dinghy.

"Somebody order a taxi?" the man chuckled.

"Sal?"

"Hop on." Sal smiled. "I'll give you a lift."

More confused than ever, Alex grabbed the side of the boat and pulled himself up. Once aboard, he was amazed to find himself sitting on the deck of a large tugboat, gripping an old fishing net. He peered around, searching for Sal.

"Over here, kid."

Alex turned. Sal now wore a purple rain slicker with a matching hat, and he was standing at the helm of the boat, steering. He tossed Alex a towel to dry off with.

"Thanks."

"No problemo." Sal smiled.

"So," Alex guessed, "is this what you meant when you said 'See you on the other side'?"

"Yep. You're my last pickup today. Hey, what time do you have?"

Alex looked at his watch, but the numbers and hands were gone. The entire face was just blue.

"Blue?" Alex said.

"Dark blue? Sky blue? Aqua blue?"

"Dark," Alex said. "Midnight blue."

"Midnight blue it is," Sal said, and he pulled a clipboard off a post. As he wrote, he spoke out loud. "Name, Alex Grindlay. Time, midnight blue. Place, the Tides of Fortune. Destination, Kismet Mountain." Sal stuck the clipboard back on its nail and explained, "Organization. It's the key to any company. We should be there pretty soon."

"Be where?"

"There," Sal restated.

"But where's there?"

"There's where we're going."

"How will we know when we get there?"

"Because we'll be there when we get there."

"Hold on," Alex moaned. "I'm so confused. What's going on here? What was that place with all the sidewalks? And who are you?"

"Me?" Sal asked. "I'm Sal. As for that place with the sidewalks, that was the station between the worlds. It's like a tunnel. And to answer your first question, that's what's going on here. You opened that fortune cookie back at the Company, and now you're on your way."

"On my way to where?"

"To your fortune."

"And?" Alex wanted a bit more information.

"The cookies will get you home. No matter what you do, make sure to read each fortune carefully. They're like your instruction manual."

"What if I just open all the cookies now? Can I go home?"

"Sorry, kiddo, but they're not designed like that."

Alex didn't believe Sal.

"Go ahead, see for yourself."

Alex pulled out a second fortune cookie and tried to split it open. No matter how hard he squeezed, it wouldn't crack. He put it on the deck and jumped up and down on it three times. But still the cookie didn't break. Alex couldn't even knock a single crumb loose.

"You can't open the next cookie until you're done here," Sal explained.

"How do I know when I'm done here?"

"When you reach The End," Sal said, "you're done."

"And how will I know when I reach The End?"

"You'll know," Sal assured him.

"What if I don't know? What if I don't reach The End?" Alex asked. "What happens then?"

"You have to reach The End. That's why you're here."

"You brought me here so that I can get out of here? That doesn't make any sense."

"Sure it does." Sal smiled. "Your fortune lies between here and The End."

"But what if I don't reach The End?" Alex asked again.

"Well," Sal insisted, "we don't want to talk about that."

"So I'm doomed."

"Now, what kind of attitude is that?"

"I've got Hoodooitis, remember."

"Of course, the Hoodooitis."

"What do you think?" Alex asked Sal. "Am I doomed, or what?"

"Only you can determine that, Alex. You're only going to get out what you put in."

"What I put into what?"

"Into the cookies. Anyway, we're here."

Alex peered out of the tugboat. There was still no sign of anything but water.

"We're where?" he asked.

"We're here," Sal repeated. "We are exactly where we are right now. Also known as *here*. And here is where you get off."

"O-O-Off?" Alex stammered. "Here? In the middle of the ocean? You're not really kicking me off your boat, are you?"

Sal nodded. "Yep," he said as he pointed to a plank sticking out from the starboard side of the tugboat.

Alex trudged across the deck, reluctantly hopped onto the plank, and turned back to Sal. "Now what?"

"Jump in."

"No way." Alex shook his head.

"It's the only way home."

"Oh well." Alex grimaced.

"Knock 'em dead," Sal encouraged.

Alex closed his eyes, braced himself for the cold water, and stepped off the plank. He landed without a splash and immediately started treading water, which looked absolutely ridiculous since he had jumped into the kitchen of a redbrick house. The ocean and Sal were both gone.

Alex stood up and scanned the kitchen. He saw pots, pans, dishes, place mats, a blender, silverware, cloth napkins—kitchen things. Nothing out of the ordinary. But Alex gasped nonetheless. This wasn't just any redbrick house, this was *his* house. This was *his* kitchen. Only the whole place was filled with somebody else's stuff.

chapter

A lex walked into the small front hallway.
"Dad?" he called out. "Dad, you still
awake?" There was no answer. Nothing unusual
there. His dad had probably fallen asleep in front
of the TV again.

He wandered up the stairs. "Dad?" he yelled.
There was still no answer. But as he crossed the
dark hallway to the closed door of his father's
room, Alex heard a welcome noise. He began to
breathe more easily as he soaked up the not-so-
melodic strains of *The Deal Wheel* theme song.
He'd never thought he would be so happy to hear
the Game Show Station.

He pushed the door open. "Dad, are you awake?"

The music stopped.

Alex gasped.

There was no sign of his dad, his dad's recliner, or his dad's TV. There was, however, a gray-and-white, curly-haired dog in round mirrored sunglasses sitting at an organ. He growled at Alex.

"Who are you being?" the dog barked.

"Um," Alex said. "Well," he continued. "You see," he explained. "It's just that . . . ," he went on.

"Wells?" the dog growled.

"Alex Grindlay," Alex finally sputtered. "I'm being Alex Grindlay. I mean, I *am* Alex Grindlay and this is my house."

"Wells, Alexgrindlay, let me tell you elsewards. This couldn't be your house, this is my house. Manfred's house!"

Alex looked around. Rugs covered the hardwood floors, and pictures of puppies hung where there had always been pictures of Alex.

"I guess you're right. This isn't my stuff," Alex admitted. "But it looks like my house, so I thought maybe you were my dad."

"Looks like?" Manfred laughed. "Looks like? Please, nothing is as it is seeming on Kismet Mountain. Bizneepers! Everypeople knows that!"

"I guess."

"So, tell me why you're here, pup."

"I'm not really sure," Alex confessed.

"How's that, exactactly?"

"Sal dropped me off here."

"Sals?"

"You don't know Sal?"

Manfred shook his head. "Nopes."

"Then why'd he drop me off here?" Alex asked, more to himself than to the dog at the keyboard.

"That's what I asked you, pup."

"Just my luck?" Alex guessed.

Manfred swept his right paw across his organ and jumped right back into *The Deal Wheel* song. Alex hummed along. The familiar music was the only thing that made sense. As soon as the dog heard him, though, he stopped playing. He looked up at Alex, shocked.

"You nose that songs?" he asked.

"Of course." Alex smiled. "Everyone knows it. It's *The Deal Wheel* song."

"Yes," Manfred howled, "yes it is!" He laughed wildly, trotted over to Alex, and waltzed the boy around the room.

"Wow," Alex remarked. "And I thought my *dad* loved that show."

"Your dad loves that show?" Manfred yelped as he took Alex for another lap around the room. "Amazers!"

"What's so amazing?" Alex asked.

"I wrote that song!" the dog finally explained.

"You did?"

"I did!" Manfred proclaimed. "Which means you mustard be Alex."

"Of course I mustard be Alex. I mean, I *am* Alex, I already told you that."

"Nopes," the dog insisted, "you were being Alexgrindlay, not Alex. But you are Alex!" Manfred restated. "I've been expectatating you."

"You have?" Alex asked. "Why?"

"Why?" Manfred yelped. "Becauses the elefant told me to! Gun of a son! He's always one hundred percent acrobat."

"You mean accurate. You've been waiting for me because an accurate elephant told you to?" Alex didn't understand.

The dog nodded. As his head went up and down, he slobbered all over himself.

"I should probably go," Alex suggested. "Um, nice to meet you and sorry to bother you." He turned toward the door.

"Nopes!" Manfred whimpered. "Don't go!"

"But I have to."

"Be staying for a song," Manfred begged. "It will explain allthings."

It was impossible to resist Manfred's puppy-dog eyes. So Alex stayed, saying, "But only for one song!"

"Fantasnic!" Manfred panted with joy and jumped onto the organ bench. "I call this song 'Lonely Dog.'" Manfred gave his head a jerk in just the right way, so that his sunglasses traveled back up his snout. Then he started to sing.

When I wokesup one loneful morn'
   so many years ago,
my li'l ones were gone, kidnappeded—why?
   I is-am don't know.
My wife she did die years before,
   and I was-am alone.

Without a friend, without a prayer,
  I pondered what to do.
I asked aroundly, "Why're we here?"
  Nopeoples had the clue,
except some grizzled ele-fant,
  a self-proclaimed guru.

"Now lettuce see," said ele-fant.
  "Your porpoise is quiet clear.
Yes, as your guru, I can say
  the reason you is here:
to write theme songs for Cypress Vine
  and allpeoples to hear."

And that, li'l pup, be what I did.
  I flopped the guru's way.
That ele-fant had told me right,
  Cypress hired me one day.
And that's how I paid for this house
  two years ago last May.

Still, life was going sidewarddown.
  Ele-fant heard my qualm
and did the thing that he done best:

he studied close my palm,
and when he figured it all out,
    he smiled and said, "Be calm.

"You is a dog," said Ele-fant,
    "that makes you man's best friend.
So, here's the skinnyful-truthness,
    this is-am not pretend:
until a boy crishplatters here,
    your pain will nose no end."

"There be no otter ways," I asked,
    "this mustard be my fate?"
Ele-fant goggled at my palm
    and started to translate.
"A boy will show, Alex his name,
    though I can't see the date."

Here I sit-sat and wondered if
    my fortuner was true,
expectatating a boy (you),
    I've thinked, thanked, thought, and stewed
'bout how I'd find what's missing-mine
    and who would start the coup.

"And there is where you have it," Manfred concluded. "Thirstful?"

Alex's head was swimming with questions. It was, after all, a rather unlikely story. He followed the dog, lugging his confused brain back down to the kitchen. Meanwhile, Manfred grabbed a juice carton out of a cookie jar and poured Alex a tall glass of orange juice. The juice became lemonade the moment it passed Alex's lips.

"So," Alex finally said, "you became a songwriter because of your palm-reading elephant friend?"

"Yes indeedly," Manfred said, tail wagging. "The same ele-fant who told me about you."

"And here I am," Alex said. He took another sip of his lemonade, only now it was cherry cola. "So what did the elephant say we should do after I showed up?"

"He said you'd help me get back my pups."

"Me?" Alex asked. "I don't think I can help you. I'm the unluckiest boy in the world. We'd better go talk to that elephant."

"Nopes. Can't do," Manfred said with a smirk. "The ele-fant be guru-ing no more."

"Why did he stop?"

"One day, while sittling around his house with little to do, he decided to read his own palm, and he learned that he had not been created for guruing."

"What was he created for?"

"Shoe salesman-ing."

"Oh."

"But he said that you'd know what to doodle, Alex."

"All I know is that I have to find The End and get out of here."

"The End, who's that?" And so Alex told Manfred all about his birthday, and Sarah Sachs (though she really had nothing to do with it, but he liked talking about her), and his dad, and Sal, and the cookies, and the moving sidewalks, and The End.

"That's quiet a day," Manfred said after he had heard everything.

Alex nodded. "Tell me about it."

"Why you?" Manfred asked.

"I'm not sure. Sal said something about it being time to change, that this is my fortune"—Alex held up the sack of cookies—"and I'm supposed to put in what I want to take out, or something like that."

"How do you *doodle* that?"

"I think you just do it." Alex was guessing now. "Something about changing the way I think about things. Looking at things sideward and backward and crossward and flippedward and upsidedownward and insideoutward."

"You mean seeing that nothing be as it is seeming?"

"Maybe. But all I really want to do is get home."

"So, let's be finding this End."

"Where should we look?"

"Out of insides, I guess." Manfred pointed out the window, past a sun-filled garden and down a grass-covered hill.

"Okay."

Manfred opened the refrigerator. There were two racks of clothes inside. He pulled out two plain white T-shirts. Then he grabbed two pairs of white sneakers out of the dishwasher. He tossed Alex a shirt and a pair of sneakers.

"Here you go," he said, "put these on."

"Why?" Alex asked.

"Be trusting me." Manfred smiled. So Alex slipped into the T-shirt and put the giant pair of sneakers over his own mismatched pair of shoes. When they were both suited up, they stepped outside.

"How strange," Alex thought. "Now it's winter out here." The sun-filled garden was nowhere to be seen. Instead, Alex and Manfred stood on the side of a mountain. It was sunny and snowing at the same time. Alex's T-shirt and sneakers had become a parka and snowshoes. But Alex was far too busy staring at the houses that littered the mountainscape to pay attention to anything else.

Every single one of the fifty or so houses on that mountain looked exactly like Manfred's house—which is to say that they all looked exactly like Alex's house. The red brick, the white shutters, the arched doorway, even the broken chimney.

There was one difference. Above Alex's front door back home, there was a flagpole that never had a flag. Every one of these houses had a flag flying from a tall flagpole. And every flag bore the same image: a woman's face. A woman with red wispy hair, solid black eyes, and brilliantly white teeth.

"Huh!" Alex gasped. "I know that woman!"

"Her?" Manfred whispered. "That's the dastardnessly Cypress Vine."

A sharp pain pierced Alex's stomach, and he let out a deep moan.

chapter

At the foot of Kismet Mountain, there was yet another redbrick house that looked just like Alex's. Only this one was the size of a castle, and like any quality castle, it was surrounded by a moat. An enormous Cypress Vine flag was flapping in the breeze. The broken chimney was lost somewhere in a sea of antennas and transmitters.

"What is that thing?" Alex asked.

"That is the Great House. It belongs to Cypress."

"What are all those antennas for?"

"Gaming shows."

Just then the Great House grew—just a little bit, but enough for Alex to notice. The flag grew, the antennas and transmitters grew, even the moat grew.

Alex rubbed his eyes. "Am I seeing things?"

Manfred shook his head. "Nopes."

"How did that happen?"

"Soft to say." Manfred threw up his front paws. "I just write the musics. All I know is this: Two or three times dailily, the Great House gets bigger. Don't know whys. Don't know hows."

"Well, what goes on in there?"

"We thinks that's where Cypress produces her gaming shows. But nopeople I nose have ever been inside."

"Really?"

"Positively."

They started trekking down the mountain. But it wasn't as easy as it seemed. Alex had never walked in snowshoes before, and he had a very hard time. First he got the front end stuck in the snow, then the back end, then both ends at the same time. And he couldn't escape the feeling that even though he and Manfred had started out by going *down* the mountain, they were now walking uphill. And the Great House, which had just been sitting at the foot of the mountain, had somehow found its way to the peak.

"I thought you said we were going down, Manfred."

"Downs and ups, what's the difference?"

"They're two different words."

"Says you. Words mean what we mean them to mean. You think down is down. Maybe I think down is up. What's the big hootinhilli?"

"How are people supposed to talk to each other if words don't mean anything?"

"But they do. Words can be meaning anything."

"That's not what I meant."

"Then you shouldn't have said it."

"I meant, how are people supposed to speak to each other if words don't always mean the same thing?"

"Oh. Wells, if that's how you want it," Manfred said as the ascent to the Great House grew steeper, "you're years too late."

"Why?"

"Becauses, allpeoples on Kismet Mountain once called spades spades, and hearts hearts, and

71

evenly clubs clubs. That was back when the mountain was one happity community. In those days, allpeoples could trust each other and allthings was exactactly as they seemed."

"What happened?"

"The dastardnessly Cypress Vine showed up. I was at a wedding. My cousin the Blue-J was marrying the beautilly Crow-bar."

"Your cousin's a blue jay?" Alex asked incredulously.

"Y knot? I was-am a Bird-dog, after all. Anyhowsers," Manfred continued, "the whole family was there. The Bird-baths, the Bird-calls, and the big fat Bird-catcher—who was wearing a golden face mask and a brand-spankily-new chest pad and baseball mitten. As the best man, the chivalrous Knight Owl received a trophy and a cash reward. The Bird of Pray stood at the head of the aisle, ready to perform the ceremony.

"Unfortunately, just as the beautilly bride made her way down the aisle (while the bridesmaids busy-nilly vacuumed her veil, dusted her bouquet, and mopped her dress), Cypress Vine came strolling in.

" 'Greetings, my friends,' Cypress snackled. She was wearing a dress of green vines, green leaves, and the minisculist scarlet flowers.

" 'Sorry to interrupt, but this will only take a minute,' Cypress screeched as she slip-sliddied down the aisle. 'Name's Cypress Vine. I just moved into town, and I know we're all going to become the most marvelous of friends. BFF,' she hissed.

" 'BFF?' the Knight Owl asked.

" 'Best Friends Forever. By the way,' Cypress hissed at the bride, 'you look great! Anyway, I won't hold up this shindig any longer. I've got boxes to unpack. I've taken the house at the peak of the mountain. Y'all just have to come in and see me sometime.' And then she turned around and left.

"The next sunup, something was different. An eerie shadow blanketed the land, a shadow from the rows and rows of antennas and transmitterers that had popped up overnight on the roof of Cypress's house. And, even strangerly, the house was bigger than it had been the day before.

"Then, a few weeks later, we all woke up to

empty houses. Every child on the mountain was missing, replaced with a small card:

Don't worry about the kids.
They're with me.
Love ya,
Cypress Vine
(your BFF)

"It was mayhemonnaise all over the mountain. We all treckled up to Cypress's house, but when we got there, we found an uncrossable moat.

" 'Cypress!' we screamed. 'Cypress!' She popped out the front door.

" 'Yes?' the witchily woman snappeled. 'Can I help you?'

" 'Give us our children back!' we demanded.

" 'Oh, I can't do that.' Cypress laughed. 'I need them. That's the problem with diabolical plans, they're so hard to pull off on your own. But don't worry, your children are all perfectly safe. And they'll stay that way, too, as long as *I'm* safe—if you catch my drift.' She winked at us, turned around, and vanished into her house.

"From that point on, Alex, nothing is as it is seeming, and all because of one woman's lies."

"Wow!" Alex empathized. "Cypress ruined my family too. My dad's so entranced by her, I can barely speak to him."

"I'm sorry, pup," Manfred soberly replied.

"Can I ask you something?" Alex went on. "If Cypress stole your kids, why do you work for her?"

"If we don't, who nose what she'll do to our li'l ones? Believe me when I tell you that I hate that witchily woman!"

"Me too," Alex agreed. "My dad hasn't stood up once since my mom died. He might as well have been kidnapped too." Just talking about his dad sitting in that chair watching TV made Alex's Hoodoo swell. "I haven't had a single lucky day in all my thirteen years."

By this time, Alex and Manfred had reached the Great House. Alex stared across the moat at the enormous Cypress Vine banners that decorated the colossal structure, and his Hoodoo swelled even more. He grabbed his stomach. "It's all her fault," he sniffled.

"Why must children always say such hurtful things?" A shrill voice intruded on their conversation. Alex and Manfred whipped around and found themselves standing face-to-face with the game show hostess with the mostess.

chapter

Alex looked up at the witchy woman. At the bone-thin neck, the red wispy hair, the black eyes, the blindingly white teeth, and the deep green dress. Only, the dress she was wearing now had scarlet accents embroidered on it. She looked bigger and scarier in person than she did on TV. From where Alex was standing, Cypress seemed to be at least eight feet tall.

She had bloodred fingernails, and she smelled rotten. Alex couldn't quite place the odor, though he thought it smelled like the opposite of Sarah Sachs's apple-blossom shampoo. Cypress smiled, and Alex shuddered.

When she took a step closer, Alex could see that she walked with a limp, since one of her legs was two inches shorter than the other. She licked her crimson lips with her slime-covered, forked tongue.

"Alex Grindlay, we meet at last." Cypress beamed. "Face-to-face, no TV screen between us. And I have my trusted composer Manfred to thank."

Manfred growled.

"How do you know who I am?" Alex asked.

"How charming, he's playing stupid—well, we can only hope he's playing, right, Manfred?"

Manfred didn't answer.

"Anywho, hon, your father has developed quite a thing for me over the years. Someone might even say that he's been completely mesmerized by my charm. But you can't blame a man for having impeccable taste, can you? Not that he's so bad-looking himself, and you can tell him I said that. Come to think of it, A—you don't mind if I call you A, do you?—I'm the closest thing to a mother you've ever had."

Alex's Hoodoo swelled up, and he forced back a tear.

"Peculiar thing." Cypress's smile grew wider. "A man and his wife go to the hospital in the still of night, but the man returns alone, with a baby in his arms."

Alex bowed his head.

"I'm sure the boy told you all about that, hey, Manfred? Real tragedy. Boy's born. Mom dies. Maybe you can write a ballad about that someday."

Again Manfred growled at the icy witch.

"We've made do, though, haven't we, A? You, your daddy, the TV, and me? Listen, hon"—she placed a finger under Alex's chin and tilted his head back up—"here's the deal. You know those cookies that crazy old Chinese man gave you? Hand 'em over."

"Cookies?" Alex said in a sniffly way. "I don't know what you're talking about."

"Playing dumb again, how clever. Look, I know you have the fortune cookies. I watched you open some of them in your father's room."

"You *could* see me!" Alex gasped. "I knew it."

"That's great, A, you're a real bright kid. Now give me the cookies."

"Nopes!" Manfred barked. "You'll never be getting home."

"Manfred," Cypress huffed as fire shot out of her mouth, "stay out of this!" She redirected her attention to Alex and smiled again. "What do you say, my boy?"

"No way." Alex shook his head, and he took several steps back, away from the monster of a woman.

"Why not?" Cypress asked. "What are you going to do with them? You have no idea where The End is. Those cookies are useless to you. If I had them, on the other hand . . ."

Cypress extended one of her lanky arms—the thing was at least four feet long—and placed it around Alex, stopping him dead in his retreating tracks. "Come on, A. I'll give you your own game show. How's that sound?"

"What do you want them for?" Alex asked.

"I'm hungry," Cypress fumed. "What do you think I want them for? I want in!"

"Into what?"

"Into your world! I've spent thirteen years sucking feebleminded humans like your father into my power, and now I want to walk among the people who worship me. Earth is ready for the reign of Queen Cypress. I just need to get there."

"That's crazy," Alex challenged.

"Is it? You ever hear of Fortune, A? That old mythical goddess who sits around in her castle way up high and spins her wheel to determine the fate of the world—talk about a great game show! And not to float my own boat, but have you ever met a more perfect host? I was born for that gig! Imagine that—me in control of everyone's fortune. Queen Cypress Vine, the goddess who holds all the strings. What a world that would be!"

"Are you insane or something?" Alex asked.

"Absolutely not!" Cypress seethed. "Think about it. You and every other person on Earth have been given the greatest gift of all—free will, the ability to determine your own fate. But you don't want it! You waste it. You sit around and wait for fate to make decisions for you. Hey, if that's the way you humans want it, I'm more than happy to provide."

"Come on, Alex," Manfred said, "we should go."

"Manfred," Cypress threatened, "you move and you're fired. As for you, A"—Cypress's long arm squeezed Alex more tightly—"you're not going anywhere until you give me what I want. I've already brainwashed much of your fate-starved world, and as soon as you let me in, the rest will fall into place."

"Then what?" Manfred asked.

"Then it's mine to control. The whole thing. No finger on Earth will move unless I command it. It's no more than any quality dictator would ask for."

"It'll never happen," Alex argued.

"It's already happening. Just look at your dad. He's mine, and you know it. The only thing stopping me from fully claiming him is one itty-bitty, impenetrable television screen. But you can get me around that, can't you?"

"What if I don't give you the cookies?" Alex asked.

"You already have." Cypress grinned. She held up the sack of cookies. Alex's eyes popped and his jaw dropped. Manfred pushed it back up for him.

"How did you do that?" Alex screamed. "That

was in my pocket." He reached into his pocket and pulled out the real sack of cookies. "What the . . . ?"

Cypress started laughing like a hyena, and as flames shot out of her nostrils, she threw her phony sack on the ground. It exploded on impact. Alex's eyes filled with thick smoke. The next thing he knew, he and Manfred were frozen in place.

"Alex," Manfred struggled to say through clenched teeth, "can you move?"

"Uh-uh," Alex moaned.

"Delightful little trick, don't you think?" Cypress skipped around them. "We've had time to come up with so many interesting things since I landed on top of this ridiculous mountain. Chemicals that make you freeze in place—no problem. Signals that transmit back and forth between the worlds—piece of cake. A conglomeration of game shows designed to hypnotize our fortune-hungry viewers—easier done than said. But we have never even come close to opening the tunnels between the worlds. We have never found a way to transmit *me*—not just my image—

to my viewers. Not until now, that is." Cypress removed the sack of cookies from Alex's frozen hand.

"Thanks a lot, A." She bent over and kissed Alex on his forehead while he stood statuelike. "No hard feelings, kid, this isn't personal. It's just your bad luck. Anyway, I have got to go. I have a world to enslave. I'll say hi to your father for you." She turned to Manfred. "Nice seeing you again, Manfred. By the way, turns out you're fired after all." And with that, Cypress skipped off toward the back of the Great House. She rounded the moat and disappeared from their sight.

A moment later Alex felt a tingle in his little toe. He was able to move it up and down. Next thing he knew, he was balling up his foot, flexing his calf, bending his knee, clenching his thigh, wiggling his butt, stretching his back, rolling his shoulders, shaking his arms, and spinning his head.

Alex looked at Manfred.

"Wells?" Manfred barked.

"Wells . . . oh well," Alex said, gripping his stomach, "looks like I'm stuck on this mountain forever."

"What's wrong with you, pup? She hasn't got away with niddily-squits yet!" Manfred took off after Cypress Vine. He screamed back, "Come on, Alex! We can still stop her!"

Feeling hopeless, Alex followed. As he ran, he tried to remind himself that nothing here was as it seemed. He was having a hard time believing it, though, until he ran straight into a wall of snow, which had arisen from the ground in front of him without warning.

"What?" Alex gasped. Three more walls of snow sprouted, and Alex was boxed in.

"It's okay," Alex told himself, "it's just snow. I can dig through it." He balled up his fist and punched at the snow wall in front of him. The wall punched him back.

Alex stumbled back into the center of his snowy prison, dumbfounded. He stared at the snow arm protruding from the wall and watched as the rest of a snowman formed. The other three walls shaped into snowmen too, and not your average friendly snowmen. Instead of carrot noses, top hats, corncob pipes, and scarves, they had jet-black eyes, steel teeth, claws, and about a four-foot advantage over Alex.

"Manfred!" Alex screamed, but Manfred had already rounded the moat and was way out of sight.

Alex looked up at the snow beasts, and his Hoodoo nearly burst. One of them winked at him, and he stumbled backward a step, planted the back of his snowshoe into the ground, and landed on his butt. Another beast picked him up by his left ankle.

"Hey!" Alex screamed as he was carried off, upside down, in the opposite direction from where Manfred, Cypress Vine, and the fortune cookies had gone. "Let go of me!" But the snow beasts didn't respond. They just trudged along. Alex squirmed and wiggled and tried to shake free, but it was no use. He was caught.

"Excuse me," he heard a familiar voice say, though he couldn't hear where it was coming from, "but if you wouldn't mind, I'd like you to put the pup down."

The snow beasts stopped trudging and turned around. And there were Manfred's hind feet! Well, that's the first thing Alex's upside-down head saw, at least. The snow beasts, on the other hand, seemed fixated on the flaming torches that Manfred held in his front paws. Manfred smiled.

What's a snow beast to do in such a situation? The beast side of him wants to attack and live up to his name. But the snow side can't escape the simple reality that he can't beat the heat. Manfred lunged forward a step. The beasts looked at each other.

"Erg?" one said in a gruff voice.

"Uhhh," responded another.

"Gurg-gurg," sputtered the third.

"Blan," decided the fourth, and they all sank back into the ground as quickly as they had formed.

"Come on!" Manfred screamed. "We can still catch her!" Alex popped to his feet and followed his friend around the moat.

The back of the mountain was nothing like the front. It was like asphalt—hot and dark. Alex ripped off his parka and snowshoes. Up ahead, Cypress Vine looked back and saw her pursuers. She upgraded from a skip to a run, heading for the one dead black tree that cut through the crimson sky.

"The tree!" Alex screamed to Manfred, who was ahead of him. Cypress was running as fast as she could, but she only had two legs, while Manfred had four. They ran down the back side of the mountain toward the dead tree, and it was only a matter of seconds before Manfred caught up with her and latched on to her right leg with his teeth.

The added weight slowed Cypress down considerably. Unfortunately, with her head start, she was only feet from the tree. Alex was running out of time. He sprinted as fast as he could. When he felt there was no time left, he jumped for it. He reached out and landed with his arms around Cypress's left leg. Then, taking his lead from Manfred, he sank his teeth into the witch.

"Get off me, you rodents!" Cypress screeched. But the second set of choppers was too much for her, and she fell forward into the tree. The big dead beast of a tree teetered over, made an awful sound, uprooted itself, and crashed down the mountain.

Carved into the ground beneath where the tree had stood was a beautifully polished rock, which seemed out of place in this dismal area. There were two words chiseled in it.

THE END.

Cypress saw the stone and smiled brightly. She removed a fortune cookie from the sack. Alex's Hoodoo swelled.

"Don't let her open that cookie!" he hollered. Manfred unlocked his jaw from around Cypress's leg and dived on top of her. Alex kicked Cypress's hand and knocked the cookie loose. It landed on the rock. The boy, the dog, and the witch all lunged after the magical dessert.

Alex reached it first, but Cypress yanked his arm behind his back and sank her knee into his neck. She reached for the cookie, but Manfred stepped on her hand. Cypress stood up suddenly, sending Manfred flying over her head. Alex, meanwhile, jumped onto Cypress's back and pulled on her red wispy hair. Yelping in pain, with Alex on her back, Cypress tottered forward and fell onto Manfred, who finally plummeted back to the ground and landed on the rock. His big, furry belly smacked right into the fortune cookie Cypress had dropped.

Life's a game that's won
or lost with a toss of
the dice.

chapter

"**G**et off me!" Cypress yelped at Alex.

"You get off me!" Manfred howled at Cypress.

Alex climbed off Cypress's back. She picked herself up off Manfred, who stood up and gave himself such a good shake that he almost fell off the moving sidewalk.

They were all standing in the station between the worlds. As they began traveling together down one of the many moving sidewalks, the colors changed from green to red to violet to yellow to orange to peach and back to green. They each took a deep breath.

"Sarah Sachs's apple-blossom shampoo," Alex said.

"Hmm, fresh liver." Manfred salivated.

"Ah, dead rats." Cypress smiled, and a single giggle slipped out of her gnarled lips. Then another, and another, and another. She sounded like a lunatic. With her black eyes lit up and her blindingly white teeth spread all the way across her face, Alex thought she *looked* like a lunatic too.

"I made it!" She was practically crying with giggly glee. "I'm in!"

"In where?" Manfred asked. "Where are we?"

"We're in the tunnel." Cypress laughed.

"We're on our way to the next world," Alex explained, sounding like an old pro at this interdimensional travel business.

"Where's that?" Manfred wondered.

"Beats me," Alex admitted. "Who has the sack of fortune cookies?"

Manfred shrugged. Alex searched his pockets. Not only did he not have the fortune cookie that had landed on the rock, or its fortune, he didn't have the sack of cookies, either.

"This is not good," he thought. He looked up at Cypress.

"What?" she spluttered.

He forced a smile. "Can I have the cookies back?"

"Don't play games with me, kid. You know I don't have them."

"Well, if I don't have them and Manfred doesn't have them and you don't have them," Alex started to yell, "who does? Huh?"

Cypress's response was so loud and so rude that it simply cannot be written here. Suffice it to say that by the time Alex, Manfred, and Cypress forked off the main sidewalk, Alex was still shocked. They headed out of the tunnel under a flashing arrow and a sign that read ALEX GRINDLAY, PARTY OF THREE.

Manfred started coughing.

"You all right?" Alex asked, but his friend couldn't answer. So Alex pounded him on his back. The slap cleared Manfred's blocked windpipe, and a tiny piece of white paper flew out of his mouth. It was the fortune. Alex grabbed it before Cypress could get her slimy hands on it.

"Give me that!" Cypress said between her teeth, and she swiped the fortune from Alex's hand right before all three of them penetrated the invisible Jello-O wall. There was an intense flash of light.

The next thing Alex knew, he was alone.

Looking around, he could only guess that he was somewhere in deep, deep, deep outer space. Stars, all around, lit up an otherwise pitch-black atmosphere. "But this can't be space," Alex thought. "I'm standing still. If this was really outer space, I'd be floating away or dying from oxygen deprivation or something."

He screamed as loudly as he could. "Hello?" He didn't really expect someone to hear him all the way out wherever he was, so he was pretty surprised when a distant voice answered.

"Hellos!"

"That's just my echo playing games with me," he told himself.

"Alex?"

"Maybe that's not my echo," he said, reconsidering.

He turned toward the voice, squinted, and saw a big ball of gray-and-white curls standing off in the distance, waving. Manfred! Alex waved back, excited. But then he had an awful thought. If Manfred had made it into this world, so too had . . .

"Yoo-hoo!" Cypress's detestable voice rattled Alex's eardrums. "Over here, hon!"

Alex and Manfred spun around. Standing off in the distance, about a hundred yards from both of them, was the deplorable woman in green. Even from that far, her evil smile almost blinded them.

"So, boys," Cypress hollered, "who's got those cookies?"

A loud POP! silenced her. A yellow flag sprang up in the center of the space between Alex, Manfred, and Cypress. The word WINNER was stenciled across it in black letters. But no one was looking at that, because hanging off the top of the flag-pole—for anyone to grab—was the missing sack of cookies.

Cypress Vine's black eyes twitched with delight. She giggled like a hyena. She even slobbered a little, also like a hyena. "Those cookies are mine!"

All three made a break for it. But none of them could move. Alex looked down. He wasn't suspended in outer space. His feet were firmly planted on a small triangular plane, which he could now see was merely the corner of a much bigger triangle. Manfred and Cypress were each stuck in one of the other two corners.

Alex tried to step out onto the larger triangle again, but his foot smacked into an invisible wall. "Ouch!" He grabbed his throbbing foot with both hands and started hopping up and down. Between hop two and hop three, something caught his eye in the space beneath him. Two words floated by as if they were caught in the currents of an invisible river. START HERE.

"Huh!" Alex gasped. "A transparent triangle," he thought. "A START HERE sign. A yellow WINNER flag flapping in the center. The fortune that said life's a game." Alex knew exactly where he was. "I'm in my Twist of Fate game—I'm in my homework!"

A sudden change in the weather made Alex

look up. A dark shadow fell over the board. Someone was sitting down to play the game. And this someone was huge. Giant! Absolutely giant! Ogre-sized, even.

Alex looked up at the massive person and couldn't believe his own eyes. He knew this giant.

"Sal?"

"Howdy, Alex," the enormous Sal answered. He waved his hand, which was ten times the size of Alex's body.

"What are you doing here?" Alex asked.

"Louie got a cold."

"Who's Louie?"

"My brother. He usually deals with things like this, but he's home sick, so here I am."

"How did you get so big?"

"I didn't. You got small."

"Oh." And then Alex said, "Can I ask you something?"

"Go right ahead." Sal smiled. "What can I do you for?"

"What happens to the two losers?" Alex asked.

"Nothing." Sal shrugged. "They get put back in the box with the rest of the game."

"So only one of us is making it out of here?"

"Afraid so," Sal confessed. "Anyway, let's get this game rolling. I have an appointment soon and I can't be late."

The gargantuan manager of the Cookie Company reached into his pocket, which seemed roughly the size of the Grand Canyon to Alex, and pulled out two humongous Styrofoam dice. One was labeled with numbers—two 1's, two 2's, and two 3's. The other had words—DOUBLE FORWARD, EVEN STEVEN, and DOUBLE BACKWARD. Alex could clearly read the dice in Sal's hand from way down on the board because they were each more than ten feet high. "Besides," he told himself, "I made them."

Sal lifted the numbered die over his head, gave it a good shake, and let it loose, causing an earthquake under the feet of the three living game pieces. The quake rippled across the board and shook the sack of cookies loose. It fell to the base of the flagpole and landed with a quiet THUD!

chapter

"It's your birthday, Alex," Sal announced. "What's your pleasure?"

"Huh?"

"You go first."

"I object!" snorted Cypress Vine.

"Overruled." Sal smiled. "You got a three, Alex. Do you want to stick or roll?"

"Why press my luck?" Alex asked himself. Three was the highest roll he could get. Sure, the other die had two DOUBLE FORWARDS on it, but Alex knew better than that. "I am the unluckiest boy in the world, after all," he thought. "I should avoid taking any chances."

"I'm gonna stick, Sal."

"Ch-Ch-Chicken!" Cypress bocked, but Alex tried to ignore her.

Sal swooped Alex up and placed him three spaces closer to the WINNER flag. Alex looked down at his new space. Not a Twist of Fate. His turn was over.

Manfred was next. Cypress, of course, objected, but Sal paid her no attention. Manfred rolled a two, took a chance, and rolled an EVEN STEVEN, which landed him on the first Twist of Fate of the game.

"What do you want, Manfred," Sal asked, "A or B?"

"A or B what?" Manfred asked.

"Choose option A or B," Alex explained. "One's Good Luck and one's Bad Luck."

"I'll be taking A," Manfred decided.

Sal picked an enormous green card off the top of an equally enormous deck that sat by the board. He flipped it over and announced, " 'Good Luck!' "

"I object!" Cypress screamed again.

Sal ignored her outburst and read the Twist of

Fate card. " 'Player advances an additional three spaces.' "

"Way to go, Manfred," Alex cheered.

"Stupid mutt," Cypress sneered.

Sal moved Manfred three spaces closer to the center.

For Cypress's turn, Sal rolled a two. When she decided to chance it, Sal rolled her a DOUBLE FORWARD, which left her one behind Manfred but one ahead of Alex.

"I'm in last place," Alex thought. "Figures." There were fifteen spaces between each player and the WINNER flag. Alex still had time to pull ahead. "But maybe if I'd chanced it, I wouldn't be losing right now," he thought as he clutched his achy stomach.

"You know, A," Cypress taunted, "I think you're going to like life inside the game box."

Sal picked up the dice.

"Remember what you learneded on Kismet Mountain," Manfred chimed in. "Nothing is as it be seeming!"

"Taking advice from a dog!" Cypress laughed. "Pathetic!"

"It truth!" Manfred yelled to Alex. "Like I told me own pup before the last round of his big checkers tournament years ago. You may be in last places, but at least you're in the game!"

"Did he win?" Cypress sneered.

"Nopes," Manfred admitted.

But Manfred was still right, and Alex knew it. After all, Cypress had tricked him into handing over the cookies on Kismet Mountain, and for a moment Alex had thought he'd end up being food for the snow beasts. But here he was. It may not have been the luckiest twist of fate, but it certainly didn't seem like the unluckiest one. He let go of his stomach.

Sal rolled a two.

"I'll chance it!" Alex screamed defiantly.

Unfortunately, the second die landed on DOUBLE BACK. Sal had to move Alex back to START HERE. Only this time, the space didn't say START HERE. It said TWIST OF FATE.

Sal took the card from the top of the deck. "A or B?"

Alex considered his options. After all, he had invented this game, right? There didn't need to be any fate involved. He could think himself out of this jam. He knew that most of the Good Lucks were A's. So that was what he decided on. "A!"

" 'Bad Luck!' " Sal shook his head, disappointed.

As Cypress Vine exploded into a fit of very unsportsmanlike cackles, the awful pain repierced Alex's stomach.

Sal read from the card, " 'Spend two turns in your waking dream.' "

"Waking dream?" Alex muttered. "I didn't write that! I don't even know what it means," he objected to Sal.

"I took some liberties." Sal smiled. "I hope you don't mind, but the gang down in marketing felt that your Twist of Fate cards needed some spicing up."

The Twist of Fate space Alex was standing on opened up like a mouth and swallowed him. The last thing he heard was Manfred barking, "Alex!" and then he found himself in a dark place, tossing around. He caught a whiff of something rancid. It smelled like . . . like potatoes and three-day-old garbage.

He heard a match strike, and when it ignited, it

illuminated a hundred elves. Alex knew exactly where he was—trapped in Odorf the Ogre's sack with the Kechish elves!

One of the tiny women stepped into the center of the group. She was wearing a crown, and Alex recognized her as the queen.

"There's still much ground to cover between here and Ogremany. We can cut a hole in the sack, unravel some of the material to use as a rope, and escape."

The king stepped forward and posed his question. "What's the point? If we escape, it will only upset the Ogres more."

A few elves nodded and grumbled, "The king's right. We don't want to anger the Ogres."

"Anger the Ogres?" the queen screamed in disbelief. "Who cares? We have to try to escape. We can't give up, we have to fight!"

The match burned out, and Alex couldn't see anything again. An elf lit another one.

"What's the point?" the king asked once more. "We're going to be beaten no matter what we do."

"Why?" the queen argued. "Why will we be beaten?"

"Because," the king explained, "we are Kechish, and in the end, all Kechish get devoured by Ogres. It is our lot."

"That's so stupid!" Alex realized this was true as soon as he said it. "Why is it your lot? Because that's what has always happened? So what? You can't just give up!" Alex went on, much to his own amazement. But nobody heard him. All they heard was the queen, who asked, "So?"

"So?" answered the king. "What's the point?"

Alex pushed his way through the elves, got right up in the king's face, and said, "You have to try to escape! Everyone's counting on you! You can't throw their lives away!"

It was useless, though. No one could see or hear Alex. The king took a step forward and walked right through him. Alex's stomach began to ache—not for his own misfortunes this time, but for the elves.

A flood of light poured into the sack. The elves screamed as Odorf's ugly face peered into his lunch bag. He licked his lips, and an enormous flood of saliva dropped onto his Kechish delicacies. As his gnarled hand reached in and scooped up some Kechish appetizers, the spot

Alex was standing on opened up and swallowed him. The last thing Alex heard was the king's futile cry, *"What have I done?"* And then Alex was spit back out onto his corner of the game board.

Two turns had passed, and Alex was back in the game. Things were looking pretty bad for him. Manfred was now only three spaces from the center of the board. But Cypress was even closer—only one space away.

"Alex!" Manfred screamed, thrilled to see his friend again.

"Sorry, hon," Cypress sympathized in a ridiculously artificial voice, "but it looks like those cookies are mine after all."

Alex sighed. He was in an awful situation. If he didn't make it to the WINNER flag in this turn, he was doomed. He knew he had lost.

Even worse, when Cypress got the cookies, Manfred would be doomed too. He and Alex would be stashed in the game's box while Cypress and the cookies were whisked away. And even worse still, she'd make it back to Alex's world, and Alex would have to live with the fact that he had personally unleashed

Cypress Vine, enslaver of humanity, on the entire human race.

The words of the Kechish king resonated in his mind. "What have I done?" Alex considered them for a minute and then asked himself, "What *have* I done? Nothing, at least not yet. Maybe I can still win," he told himself. "After all, nothing is as it seems, and life's a game that's won or lost with a toss of the dice, right?"

With all that said, any way you cut it—win or lose—this was Alex's last turn. He looked up at Sal. "Toss the dice!"

The first die fell. The board quaked. When it stopped, Sal boomed, "Three."

To which Alex impulsively answered, "Chance it, Sal!"

The second die fell. DOUBLE FORWARD.

The six-space move presented Alex with yet another option. He landed on a Twist of Fate space. "A or B?" Sal asked with something of a smile.

"A!" Alex confidently shouted.

"A." Sal read from the card, " 'Good Luck!' "

"You're gonna need it, twerp!" Cypress snapped.

Manfred barked at her.

" 'Roll the first die and move three times the new roll.' "

Sal let it fly. The die tumbled over and over until it smacked right into Cypress Vine and pinned her to the ground. "Three!" Sal announced, and he left the die on top of Cypress.

"Three times three is nine," Alex quickly figured out, "and nine plus six is fifteen, and there are only fifteen spaces, which means . . ."

Sal picked up Alex and moved him to the center of the board. Alex had won the game!

He picked up the sack of cookies, and the letters on the flag flapping above his head rearranged themselves to spell out THE END.

He looked out across the board and took a much-needed deep breath. If he opened a cookie now, Manfred would be stuck in the game box with Cypress Vine. But before his Hoodooitis had a chance to start acting up again, Alex assured himself, "I made it this far, I can get both of us out of here!"

"I love this!" Cypress proclaimed as she wriggled out from beneath the die. "You can go, A, but you have to leave Manfred behind with me. This is great!"

Alex looked down at the cookies in his hand. "There has to be another way out of this," he said. "Think!" he yelled to himself. "Look at it sideward and flippedward."

"Goes!" Manfred howled.

Cypress's crooked smile danced on her face. Her black eyes twinkled with glee. "Yeah," she taunted, "go on and open it! Don't worry about Manfred." She flashed her bloodred nails. "I'll take care of him."

Alex looked up at Sal.

"Time's running out," warned the giant.

On the yellow flag above Alex's head, THE END was beginning to fade. The word WINNER was reappearing.

Alex tilted his head sideways and looked back over at Manfred. "Ha!" This time he was seeing things differently. He looked at Manfred and pictured himself as a pitcher lining up with his catcher. Alex grabbed a cookie from his sack. As he held it over his head with his left hand, THE END all but vanished.

He cocked his right hand behind him and sent it flying over his head, breaking the cookie in his left hand in half—leaving one half in his hand and throwing the other half clear across the board, just as he had pitched a ball hundreds of times during six years of Little League. And then he was gone.

To reach the foot
of the mountain,
you must enter the mouth
of the volcano.

chapter

Once again, Alex was heading down a moving sidewalk in the station between the worlds. Another one of his favorite songs was playing at a perfect volume, and it smelled the way Sarah Sachs did when she sat behind him in class. The colors of the worlds changed around him.

He looked around desperately, but there was no sign of Manfred. The sidewalk next to him was moving in the opposite direction. "I wonder if I can go back. It's only three or four feet away. Maybe I could jump it."

But then there was a flash of light, and next thing Alex knew, something was licking his face.

"Manfred! You made it!" Alex reveled in the dog's slobber. "You made it!"

"You bet-ya!" Manfred's tail was wagging like crazy. "That was amazers back there, pup."

"What happened?" Alex asked.

"Wells," Manfred explained, "after you disappeared, the second half of the cookie landed by me front paw. It was a perfectitious throw."

"Thank you. I play baseball," Alex explained modestly.

"You're welcome. Anyhowsers, the whole thing was great. When the cookie floppsied down by me paw, Cypress Vine's smile disappeared. She plegged and beaded me to share my half. But I just shook my head. And smiled. She offered to put me in charge of the entire music department for all of her gaming shows—the whole kat and kipoodle! But I just kept smiling, and I told her that she'd already fired me. Then I crishplattered that cookie with my paw. With Cypress trapped back there on the gaming board, you'll be home before you know it. Maybe we'll even find my pups."

Another flash of light interrupted them. The

light was gone as quickly as it had come. But it left someone behind. Cypress Vine.

"Surprise!"

"What?" Manfred screamed. "How did—"

"You should have been a little more gentle with that cookie." Cypress grinned. "You sent an army of crumbs over my way."

"Bizneepers!" Manfred grimaced. "We can't break a catch."

But then ALEX GRINDLAY, PARTY OF TWO appeared in the air above their heads. Though Alex and Manfred broke away from the sidewalk, Cypress was left behind.

"Come back here!" Cypress squealed. "Come back here!"

Alex held up the sack of cookies for Cypress to see. He swung them back and forth like a hypnotist's watch. A flash of light consumed him and Manfred, and they pushed through another wall of invisible Jell-O.

They materialized in a large, wet, vibrating, pinkish cave. It was dark. The ground beneath their feet was wet and slick and constantly undulating. Alex had a hard time balancing himself. Luckily, large bumps covered the entire surface and gave him something to hold on to. Alex breathed in, and his head filled with mentholated air. The entire place smelled minty fresh.

Alex took a cautious step forward and felt the ground under his feet give, ever so slightly. It was like walking on a mattress—a sprawling, pinkish, bumpy mattress. Light flooded one end of the cavern, and the words, "I'm gonna kill him!" echoed throughout the entire place as Alex and Manfred were nearly knocked over by a sudden blast of air.

The light abruptly disappeared as the opening closed, and Alex remembered the fortune. He held it out for Manfred to read.

TO REACH THE FOOT OF THE MOUNTAIN,
YOU MUST ENTER THE MOUTH OF THE VOLCANO.

"What's it mean?" Alex asked.

"I don't nose," Manfred admitted.

There was another flood of light, and this time the words "I swear, that kid's dead!" echoed all around them as a second blast of air knocked Alex off his feet.

"What is that?" Manfred asked.

Squinting into the light, Alex could see the entrance to the cave. It was partially obstructed by large white rocks. The entrance closed, and the light disappeared again.

"Those aren't rocks," Alex realized.

"Of course they're not!"

Alex and Manfred spun around. A frumpy little man with big ears, small eyes, a medium-sized nose, and a ridiculously thick mustache that hid his mouth stood behind them. He wore knickers, suspenders, and a strange headdress—an eyeball hat. It covered his entire head, except for a small cutout for his face. "They're teeth," the man said. "Whoever heard of rocks in a mouth?"

"We're in a mouth?" Manfred nearly passed out.

"That explains the minty-fresh scent." Alex had finally placed it. "I think I use the same brand of toothpaste!"

"We're in somepeople's mouth?" Manfred hollered.

"Follow me," the man with the eyeball headdress instructed. He turned around and started walking across the large pink tongue. "Not bumps. Taste buds!" Alex exclaimed.

Alex looked at Manfred. "What should we do?"

Manfred shook his head. "Pup, I'm downright flabberwildered." So they followed the strange man.

They hiked across the tongue, through an opening created by the two teeth on either side of a missing premolar. Then they took a left and wandered through the ravine between the gum line and the inner lining of the cheek.

There was a small panel with a button on it stuck to the cheek's lining, back by the tonsils. Their guide pressed this button. "It'll only be a second," he assured Alex and Manfred.

One Mississippi . . . DING!

Elevator doors that blended seamlessly into the lining of the cheek opened. The man with the eyeball on his head hopped into the elevator car. Alex and Manfred followed, flabbergasted. Their odd guide pressed another button. The elevator doors closed and they started to go up.

"Hello, hello," said the man as he grabbed Alex's and Manfred's hands. "Nice to make your acquaintance. Popper's the name."

"Alex," Alex said.

"Manfred," added Manfred.

"I know. You're from the outside."

Alex and Manfred didn't know what that meant.

"From the board game; well, most recently," Popper rambled on. "I mean, Manfred, we've known you for years. We all really love your music."

"Th-Thanks," Manfred stammered, completely confused.

"And, Alex, we've been watching you for what, thirteen years now? You and your dad, I mean."

"What?" Alex said. "What do you mean, watching?"

"You know. Watching. As in looking at with one's eyes." Popper chortled.

"How?" Alex asked.

"How? I work in the Left Eye, that's how."

There was another DING! and the elevator doors opened again.

"Speaking of which"—Popper gestured outside the small elevator car—"here we are."

Alex and Manfred stepped into a large spherical room. There were legions of other frumpy little people with eyeball hats, sitting with their backs to Alex and Manfred at sophisticated consoles and computers. They were focusing on the darkly tinted glass wall of the sphere directly in front of them.

"Welcome to the Left Eye," Popper said.

"Thanks," Manfred sort of whimpered.

Alex didn't say a word. He was too busy staring through the glass wall. He couldn't believe what he was seeing—the moving sidewalks in the station between the worlds. As they moved by in every direction, the colors kept changing—first green, then red, then violet, then yellow, then orange, then peach. The voice echoed again. "When I see that kid . . . Urg!" and the entire eyeball room quaked.

The spherical window shifted down, and Alex could now see a pair of leather sandals sticking out of the bottom of a green dress with scarlet accents.

"Oh no!" He steadied himself on Manfred's shoulder. "We're inside Cypress Vine!"

chapter

Upon hearing Alex's revelation, Manfred passed out, and Alex almost fell on top of him. As Popper tried to wake Manfred, Alex tried to come to grips with the fact that he was inside Cypress Vine's left eyeball. "I've had my share of crazy adventures tonight," Alex sputtered, "and I think I've handled everything okay—talking dogs, disintegrating fields, killer snowmen, whatever. But this, I don't know."

Just then Manfred came to, looked around, and passed out again. Upon coming to a second time, he promptly passed out a third time. At which point several other little fellows with eyeball headresses ran over carrying red buckets labeled TEARS.

"Ready?" the leader of the bucket-toting eyeball brigade screamed. His underlings poised their buckets. "One, two, three."

SPLASH!

The sudden deluge of salty water managed not only to wake Manfred but also to keep him from passing out again.

"Nice work, boys," Popper shouted after the retreating team. Then he added to Alex, "They're in Tears."

"Yeah," Alex said, "I figured." He turned to Manfred. "Are you okay?"

Manfred gave himself a good shake and dried off. "Am I okay? Nopes! I'm not okay! I'm inside the witchily woman who kidnapped my pups!" He marched over to the window of the eyeball and punched it.

"Ouch!" Cypress cried, and the entire eyeball room quaked again. Manfred looked back at Popper. "Okay, wee-friend, tell me something. How do we get out of inside of here?"

"Well," Popper considered, "there are so many different ways to get out of Cypress. You could go through a tear duct, a sweat gland, the eardrum, a cut . . ."

"How about a foot?" Alex asked.

"Hmmm," Popper said. "I guess you could sneak out somewhere down there."

"Yuk!" Manfred growled. "Not me. I say we take the first abominable exit."

"But we need to get to The End," Alex asserted, "and that's at the foot of the mountain."

"In that case," Popper advised, "you two are going to want to catch the H train. It'll take you down to the heart, and you can transfer to a downtown bus from there."

A loud whistle blew.

"Oh!" Popper piped. "Looks like my break is over." All the eyeball workers sitting at the consoles packed up their things, cleared space for the next shift, and filed out. Popper sent Alex and Manfred on their way, instructing them to follow the eyeballed masses over to the train station in Cypress's nose.

The station was packed with more frumpy little fellows—hundreds of them. Some of them wore eyeballs on their heads, but most of them wore noses. There were also people with feet where their heads should be, and lungs, and femurs and tibulas and knees and ears and kidneys and stomachs, and Alex even saw one or two intestine-heads.

Eventually a train pulled up, and Alex and Manfred squeezed into one of the cars.

As the doors closed, a voice came over the speakers. "This is an express train. Next stop, Epiglottis!"

Alex and Manfred both giggled.

A few minutes later the train pulled into the Epiglottis. The doors opened and everyone piled off the train. Then the doors slammed shut and the train pulled out of the station.

"Um, Alex," Manfred pointed out to Alex, who was busy studying a map on the wall, "there's nopeoples left on this train."

Alex looked around. He and Manfred were the only two commuters left. The others had hurried off so quickly that they'd left all sorts of things behind. Newspapers hung on the backs of empty seats. An umbrella rolled back and forth on the floor. A briefcase leaned up against a pole. Someone had even left his pants behind. It felt like a ghost train.

The conductor's voice came over the speakers again. "Next stop, Hoodoo!"

Alex didn't quite know how to respond, though his Hoodoo did. He clutched his stomach in horrendous pain. He looked back at the map.

"I don't get it," he said to Manfred. "The H train is supposed to stop at the Heart, not at the Hoodoo."

"Wells," Manfred responded, "that explainers it," and he looked up at a sign. "We're not on the H, we're on the H-1."

"We have to stop this train." Alex was panicking. He started walking quickly toward the front of the car.

"Where we going?"

"To talk to the engineer."

Alex and Manfred hopped from car to car, eventually making their way up to the front. They banged on the engineer's door, but there was no answer. Alex tried kicking it down. But the door didn't budge. So he tried the handle. It was unlocked.

"Well, what do you know?" Alex blushed.

There was only one problem now. There was no one inside the booth.

"Hey now," Manfred asked, "who's driving this train?"

"*That* is," Alex figured. He pointed at a computer sitting inside the tiny room. "It's automatic." He turned back to Manfred. "Oh well. I guess we're going to the Hoodoo."

"And what exactactly *is* the Hoodoo?"

"The Hoodoo is the place where bad things come from."

"Wells, that would explain why allpeople hoppled off at the last stop, wouldn't you say?"

"Yeah."

The train started to slow down. Alex shook his head. It pulled into a dark station. The tunnel was as purple as it could be without being black. The train doors opened, and the computerized conductor announced, "Last stop! Everybody out!"

Alex stepped out first. He looked down the empty platform. There was no sign of anyone else. It seemed as if no one had been through the place in years. When Manfred stepped out of the train, all the doors shut, but the train didn't move—it just sat there.

The entire tunnel was a deep violet color, except in one spot. A red light pulsed faintly, way off in the distance. "Let's go this way," Alex suggested, though he found it hard to take the first step with his knees knocking so hard. Manfred found it twice as hard, since he had twice as many knees.

The red light turned out to be a red exit sign. It was right above a spiraling stairwell that twisted down. A small neglected sign read TO HOODOO, pointing the way.

Alex looked back down the platform for an alternative. But there were no other exits, and the train didn't look as if it was planning on moving anytime soon.

"After you?" Alex asked his friend.

Manfred shook his head. "No way! Your unfortunate cookie brought us here, pup. You go first."

"Fine." Alex took a deep breath, gathered his courage, straightened his shoulders, stuck out his chest, took another deep breath, re-collected his courage, took another deep breath . . .

"Wells?" Manfred tapped his foot. "What's with the dallydillying?"

One more quick but deep breath, and Alex headed down the stairs. He clutched the handrail, sweat dripping from his palms. The stairs seemed to go on forever, the same deep violet color as the walls and the floor and the ceiling; there was no telling where anything stopped and where anything else started.

"What you think is down there?" Manfred asked.

"Honestly?"

Manfred had to think about that for a moment. "Yeah, I guessen so."

"It's going to be horrible and ugly and gruesome. Like a giant tumor," Alex guessed. "You know, I once saw a four-hundred-pound tumor on TV."

"Four hundred pounds? Bizneepers! You mustard be kidding."

"Really," Alex insisted. "It had hair in it, and teeth and bone fragments, and it was shiny and deformed and disgusting. That's what the Hoodoo's like—only it's uglier."

"Oh." Manfred gulped. "Sorry I asked."

They continued for a few more twists, as the purple walls took on an iridescent glow. Finally Alex could see the last step a few feet below.

The staircase left Alex and Manfred on top of a

platform, which was suspended in the middle of an otherwise empty ball. Alex felt as if he were standing inside a huge purple balloon.

A little man with a purple ball on his head slept in an old beat-up lawn chair at the end of the platform. He was clutching a pen, and in his lap he had a book of crossword puzzles opened to a drool-covered page.

"Excuse me," Alex quietly said. The man did not stir. "Excuse me," Alex tried again, a little more loudly.

"Hey, wee-man!" Manfred yelled. "Wake up!"

The man awoke with such a start that he fell out of his chair. He popped up, shook off his sleep, and hugged Alex and Manfred. After a few moments it was clear that he wasn't planning on letting go.

"Um," Alex said. "Excuse me."

"Let go of us!" Manfred barked.

The man stepped back. "So sorry. So sorry. I'm Zipper. It's been so long since anyone has come around, and I'm just so happy to see you two."

"Of course no one comes down here," Alex said. "Who wants to go to the Hoodoo?"

"What's wrong with the Hoodoo?" the man with the Hoodoo hat asked. "Why wouldn't you want to come here?"

"Isn't it obvious?" Alex asked. "I mean, just take a look at . . ." But there was nothing to take a look at. No cancer; no tumors; no teeth, hair, or bone fragments. Nothing. It was just empty space. "This *is* the Hoodoo, isn't it?"

"Yes."

"Where's all the bad stuff that comes from here?"

"I'm sorry to disappoint you, friend, but there's nothing bad here."

"Of course there is," Alex insisted. "All bad things come from the Hoodoo!"

"Take a look." The little fellow gestured around the room. "It's just me, my book, and the pump." He pointed over the side of the platform at the bottom of the sphere. An old hand pump sat on the ground.

"Then how does the Hoodoo make bad things happen?" Alex asked.

"It doesn't." Zipper shrugged. "It helps prevent them."

"I don't understand. I thought—"

"The same thing everyone else thinks," Zipper interrupted, clearly frustrated. "But no one comes around to see for themselves."

"See what for themselves?" Alex asked.

"It's like this," the purple-headed fellow said. "You know when you do something wrong, or something bad happens to you, or you're frightened or nervous?"

Alex and Manfred both nodded.

"And you know how whenever you get into any of those situations you get that pain right on top of your stomach?"

"Yes!" Alex almost shouted.

"Well, that pain is your Hoodoo swelling up."

"I know!" Alex interjected. "That's what I was saying."

"But you don't understand. When most people are about to do something wrong, or when something bad is about to happen to them, or they're frightened or nervous, someone up there"—he pointed straight up, toward the brain—"sends a message down here. Then some schmo like me starts pumping the Hoodoo full of air."

"Why?" Alex asked.

"Because the Hoodoo, as you may know, sits

right above the stomach. When it's inflated, it pushes into the top of the stomach."

"And that's where the pain comes from. So how does the Hoodoo make things happen?"

"The Hoodoo's not the cause of the trouble. The pain is a signal that there is, has been, or will be trouble. Now, what kind of trouble, that's hard to say. You see, there's no reason to fear the Hoodoo. In fact, a little appreciation might be nice. All it's doing is looking after you."

Manfred was puzzled. "So nothing bad comes from here?"

"Nope." Zipper smiled. "It's just a ball of air."

Alex smiled. "And it's *good* for you?"

"Yup. It's the *broken* Hoodoos you have to look out for," Zipper added.

"What's that mean?" Alex asked.

"Take Cypress, for instance. She's a witch, right?"

Alex and Manfred were both quick to agree.

"Did you ever wonder what makes her so mean?"

"No."

"Faulty wiring. No pump order has ever been sent down here from anyone upstairs. So Cypress never knows when she's acting evil because, with a busted Hoodoo, she's incapable of feeling pangs of guilt, remorse, fear, accountability—you name it."

"That's why she'll never change her dastardnessly ways," Manfred suggested.

"And you know what happened to the lady who never changed," Alex asked, "don't you, Manfred?"

"Nopes."

"She stayed the same."

"And that's that." Zipper smiled. "You guys care to join me in a crossword puzzle?"

"No thanks," Alex declined. "We have to head down to the foot." He smiled.

"Well," Zipper sighed, "it was nice meeting you both. Maybe when you're back out there"— he pointed up the spiraling stairs—"you can start spreading the skinny on the Hoodoo. And if you ever find yourselves in Cypress again, stop on by."

"Sure thing," Alex said as he started back up the stairs.

"See ya around, wee-Hoodoo-head," Manfred yelled, but Zipper's purple noggin was already buried in his book of crosswords.

chapter

13

Alex and Manfred climbed back up to the purple train station. It was even more empty
than when they had left it—not only were there
no people waiting for the train, there was no
train. But this time they weren't afraid.

"Maybe we should bidaddle back to the Hoodoo and ask Zipper for a map," Manfred suggested.

"Hold on a sec." Alex gasped. "Look."

A manhole-sized ray of red light glowed beside the staircase to the Hoodoo. It came from
a hole in the ground, which hadn't been there
before.

"And look at that." Manfred pointed.

In the red light, Alex and Manfred could now see that the word DOWN was written vertically in large yellow letters on the wall of the tunnel. The bottoms of the letter N had been finished off with arrows that pointed deeper into the hole.

"What is it?" Manfred wondered.

Alex stared into the tunnel. "It looks like a water slide."

"Where's it go?"

"Down," Alex guessed.

"And I suppose that you want to slip-sliddle down it?"

"Well, we do need to get to the foot, and the foot is down. So . . ."

"Pups." Manfred shook his head.

"See you at the bottom!" Alex hopped into the tube and slid out of Manfred's sight. Manfred pinched his nose, closed his eyes, and jumped in after his friend.

Alex whipped through the tube at an astounding speed. His eyes, wide open, were completely dried out by the rushing winds. Shooting along faster and faster, he whooped with excitement. Manfred whooped too, but for different reasons.

He was trying to slow himself down, but the tube was too slippery for that.

They slid and twisted and corkscrewed and looped and banked and dropped straight through Cypress Vine, who had no idea that any of this was going on inside her.

Alex flipped over and started flying headfirst down the slide. "If only Sarah Sachs could see me now, water-sliding through a witch!" he thought. "She wouldn't believe her eyes!" He whizzed through a series of corkscrew turns and screamed up to Manfred, "Isn't this great?"

"Nopes!" Manfred howled.

One more turn, one more bump, one more twist, one more hump, and then SMASH! Alex flew out the end of the tube and smacked right into something. Manfred smacked into him a second later. They were inside Cypress's big toe. They could tell because the moment they landed, several little fellows wearing big toes on their heads ran over to make sure they were all right.

While assuring the toe-heads that he was fine, Alex was distracted by a horizontal sliver of light. He had a sneaking suspicion that the crack was actually the small space between the tip of Cypress's big toe and the edge of her big toenail.

"There," Alex said, pointing up at the light. "That's where we're going. The End has to be out there."

They said good-bye to the toe-heads and crawled out under the nail. Alex's head popped out first, then his arms. He grabbed hold of the well-manicured edge of Cypress's big, big toenail and pulled the rest of himself up onto its nail-polished platform, as if he were doing a chin-up. He reached back down and helped Manfred scuttle up.

"Here we are," Manfred said. "The foot of the mountain."

"Keep your eye out for The End," Alex said. "It's got to be around here somewhere."

They hiked across the toenail, climbed over two sandal straps, and hit the ankle. There was nowhere left to go.

"Wells?" Manfred asked.

Alex looked around. "The End has to be here. The fortune said so."

"Maybe we're on the wrong foot," Manfred suggested, but Alex didn't hear him.

Alex perked up and told Manfred to look down.

His curly-haired friend was standing on a patch of freckles that spelled out the words THE END.

"Well, well, well," a voice boomed at that very moment. "What have we here?" Cypress's planet-sized head descended upon the minuscule Alex and Manfred. "Aren't you the two most peculiar-looking insects I've ever seen?" Alex was staring straight into Cypress's eye—and it was twelve times his size.

"Alex!" Manfred screamed. "Open a cookie!"

Alex reached into his pocket. He yanked at the sack of cookies, but it snagged on the lining of his pants.

"Oh no you don't," Cypress boomed, and she blew air onto Alex and Manfred. The hurricane-force gale picked them up and tossed them about like a feather caught in the wind. Though he was only traveling up Cypress's leg, in his ant-sized state it felt to Alex as if he were floating up something as tall as the Eiffel Tower. And what an exhilarating feeling that was. Right beneath Cypress's knee, Alex latched on to the folds of her green dress. Manfred landed below him.

"Where are you two?" Cypress's tremendous voice thundered. She was scanning the sidewalk, searching for her bug-sized nemesis carrying the sack of magical fortune cookies.

Meanwhile, the nemesis and his friend were busy unraveling the scarlet threads that accented Cypress's deep green dress. In their tiny hands, the thread was as strong as climbing rope.

"Are you positilly this will work?" Manfred asked.

"No," Alex admitted. "Up until today, I've been the unluckiest boy in the world, so chances are it won't work. But what other choice do we have?"

They continued to unravel the thread.

"You better show yourselves," Cypress threatened, "before I accidentally step on you."

Alex shuddered at the awful thought. "If I make it through this," he told himself, "I'll never step on a bug again."

"Incoming!" Manfred screamed as Cypress's gargantuan head nose-dived toward them. Manfred tucked himself behind a fold in the green velvet. Alex buried himself inside a pocket of embroidered scarlet stitching and peered out.

141

Cypress's enormous face appeared upside down in front of him. He could see inside one of her huge nostrils.

"She really needs to blow her nose," Alex thought. Cypress pulled up a little, and he looked straight into one of her giant eyes. He held his breath and imagined how it was going to feel when she pinched him between her thumb and index finger and then popped him like a zit. The awful thought aggravated his Hoodoo. It might just have been trying to help him, as Zipper had said, but at the moment it certainly hurt.

Cypress's head retracted. She hadn't seen them. Alex and Manfred both took a much-needed breath.

Alex looked over to Manfred. "You ready?"

"Yes! On three!"

"One!"

Alex stuck the next fortune cookie in his mouth.

"Two!"

He grabbed on to the top of his rope-thread and let the rest fall down to Cypress's foot.

"Three!"

Alex and Manfred both pushed off Cypress and

started sliding down the rope. They whizzed down her leg at an awesome speed. Manfred crashed into the freckle patch first, and Cypress felt him land.

"There you are!" she hollered, spying Alex, who was dangling off her dress like a spider. As she reached to pluck him off, Alex did the only thing he could. He let go of his rope and jumped, plummeting right into Manfred. The last thing he saw was Cypress's thumb and index finger closing in on him. But by the time the two immense digits met, Alex had already taken a bite out of the cookie, and he and Manfred were gone.

Sometimes the only way
out is in.

chapter

The moment Alex bit the cookie, he and Manfred shot up to their full sizes. Cypress was still hunched over looking for them, and Alex's head knocked right into her nose. As she jerked back and grabbed her throbbing schnoz, she kicked Manfred off her foot.

She quickly recovered from Alex's and Manfred's sudden growth spurts, grabbed Alex by his ear, and pinched it tightly. "I've had enough of your nonsense, sweetheart. Give me the cookies."

"No." Alex winced, and cookie crumbs shot out of his mouth. "Let go of me!"

"Not until I get what I want," she screeched,

and she stepped down on Manfred's head, pin-
ning the dog's mug to the surface of the moving
sidewalk. Stuck together in this configuration,
Alex, Manfred, and Cypress forked off beneath a
blinking neon arrow labeled ALEX GRINDLAY, PARTY
OF THREE.

"What?" Cypress screamed. "What are we doing *here*?" In a fit of anger, she let go of her prisoners so that she could more effectively flail about
and pout. Alex clutched his throbbing ear and
slowly opened his eyes, which until then had been
squeezed shut in pain.

"What *are* we doing here?" he wondered, looking out over Kismet Mountain. He, Manfred, and
Cypress were across the uncrossable moat. They
were standing in the snow outside the entrance to
Cypress's Great House. Well, Alex and Manfred
were standing. Cypress was still hopping up and
down, enraged.

"Why are we going flippety-flopward?" Manfred whispered to Alex. "What are we doing back
on Kismet Mountain?"

"Let's find out," Alex suggested, and he peeled
the soggy fortune off his tongue.

As always, the fortune didn't seem to make any sense. Unfortunately, Alex and Manfred were so distracted for the moment that they did not see Cypress Vine standing several feet behind them. They did not know that she had stopped dancing around like a brat and that she was beaming with joy. Her black eyes were locked on the snow-covered ground by Alex's foot. The last cookie had fallen out of his pocket and landed in the snow without a sound. Alex hadn't noticed.

By the time Alex and Manfred heard her coming, it was too late. In one swift move, Cypress scooped up the cookie from the ground and snagged the fortune from Alex's hand. She read the fortune and smiled so widely that Alex could practically see into her stomach. "Well, if you two darlings will excuse me now, I think I'll be heading *in*." She slipped through the front door into the Great House.

Alex ran for the door, but it slammed shut in his face, almost taking off his nose. He tried the handle, but it was locked. At the same moment, the Great House grew, ever so slightly, but enough to bump Alex and knock him off his feet. He could hear Cypress's laugh echoing from inside. She made him so angry that he stood up and bashed his fist against the front door.

"Calm down, Alex. There mustard be another way in."

Alex stared at Cypress's castle-sized version of his house back home. The red brick, the white shutters, the arched doorway, and the broken chimney lost somewhere up in that sea of antennas and transmitters. "Of course!" he screamed. "Come on!" He ran off, Manfred on his heels.

Around the side of the house, way off toward the back, was a Bilco hatch—one of those metal cellar doors that jut out from a house and open on the outside. Alex's house was identical to each of the houses on Kismet Mountain in all ways but one: size. The way he figured it, size had nothing to do with the facts that he had broken the lock on his cellar door way back when he was ten years old and that no one had bothered to fix it. So the cellar locks on all these houses must be broken too. He grabbed the handle of one of the massive

Bilco hatch doors and gave it a good tug. He was right. The lock was busted.

Alex and Manfred descended the stairs into the cellar of the Great House.

"You nose"—Manfred's voice trembled a bit— "in all the years I've been working for Cypress, I've never been inside here. And to tell you the truth, I've never wanted to be inside."

"It's not that bad, Manfred. I mean, you've already been inside Cypress today—how much worse can it be inside her house? Besides, even if she didn't have the last cookie, The End is in here. So the only way out for me is in."

They stepped into the cellar. Green light, from green lightbulbs, showered the vast room.

"Look at all this stuff," Alex marveled. The cellar was filled with game wheels and buzzers and score cards and curtains and prizes and game boards and microphones and every other sort of prop you could possibly need on any sort of game show. Alex recognized things from *The Deal Wheel, The Puzzle Pyramid, The Crazy Clue Course Challenge, The Nice Price,* and every other one of his dad's favorite shows.

Alex and Manfred rifled through a few boxes and snooped around for a few moments before Manfred's ears suddenly perked up.

"Shhh!" he warned. "Listen," he whispered. There was the *du-dump, du-dump, du-dump* of a noise approaching. Someone was coming down to the basement.

"Quick," Alex mouthed, "hide." He and Manfred squeezed behind one of the gigantic special-edition Deal Wheels. Crouched between the Very Special Christmas Prize Package Wheel and the Great Groundhog Day Getaway Wheel, Alex watched as the footsteps grew louder. Cypress Vine stepped into the light.

She rummaged through a box of props, and Alex considered rushing her to recover the lost cookie. But before he could signal to Manfred, Cypress pulled her head out of the box, walked back toward the steps, and yelled, "Hey! I can't find it!"

"Hold on!" another shrill female voice answered. A rapid series of *du-dumps* echoed above Alex's and Manfred's heads as another woman ran down the steps to join Cypress. When this woman stepped into the light, Alex saw that she had solid black eyes, red wispy hair, brilliant white teeth, and a slender neck that disappeared into a deep green dress.

She was Cypress Vine too.

Alex and Manfred looked at each other, absolutely bewildered. Alex was about to say something, but Manfred covered his friend's mouth.

The second Cypress quickly found what her twin had been looking for, a large clear briefcase filled with fake hundred-dollar bills. The wicked twins turned around and marched back upstairs.

"Did you see that?" Alex asked.

"Yes." Manfred's teeth were chattering. "She can multiplify."

But Alex wasn't buying that explanation. "Did you notice anything different about those two Cypresses?"

"Nopes." Manfred shrugged. "Only that there were two of them."

"There was no scarlet on their dresses. And they looked shorter than the other one. Come to think of it, they looked more like the game show hosts my dad watches all day."

"What are you saying?" Manfred asked.

"I'm saying that I don't think either of those women is Cypress Vine."

"Then who are they?"

"Clones?" Alex suggested.

"So where is the real Cypress?"

"Up there." Alex pointed.

Manfred reluctantly followed his friend. At the top of the stairs, they stopped dead in their tracks all over again. This place was not what they'd expected. Unlike Alex's and Manfred's homes, the Great House was one gigantic room. No kitchens, hallways, living rooms, or even separate floors. Just one cavernous space. Nearly every single inch of every single wall and of the entire ceiling was covered in TV monitors. And on each monitor, different men and women stared straight ahead with blank expressions. In the middle of the wall facing Alex and Manfred, there was a black sign with giant red numbers: 2,748,312.

The floor was covered with game show sets. There must have been thirty shows set up, and they were all taping. The Great House was nothing more than an enormous television studio. Clones of Cypress Vine stood in the centers of the sets, hosting. Their shrill voices hurt Alex's head.

"Hello, I'm C. C. deVine, and this is *The Puzzle Pyramid!*"

"Welcome to *The Crazy Clue Course Challenge*. I'm your host, Cy P. Vine!"

"Thanks for tuning in to *The Nice Price*. I'm C. P. Veene!"

"It's time for *The Deal Wheel* with me, your host, Cyp V. Ine!"

There were at least three television cameras taping each game show. And for every camera, there was another clone operating it. Off to the side of each show, there were even more clones. They were slipping normal, everyday clothing over their green dresses and hiding their evil faces behind masks of average-looking folks. When a host introduced her contestants, the disguised clones would run onto the stage. Everyone, the hosts as well as the phony contestants, read all their lines off cue cards, which were held up by more clones.

"It's all fixed!" Alex gasped. "There's no chance involved. The game shows are lies. The contestants aren't even human! They're Cypresses."

155

There were seven loud DING!s. The last 2 in the giant red 2,748,312 flipped over. It now read 2,748,319. Then seven more TV screens, along with seven more loyal viewers, appeared. The entire house magically grew just enough to make room for the new monitors.

"Did you see that?" Manfred asked.

"I th-think so," Alex stammered.

"There mustard be a thousand clones in here. How are we going to find the real Cypress?" Manfred asked.

"Oh," a shrill voice interrupted, "I don't think it's going to be that difficult." Alex and Manfred twirled around. Five clones stood between them and the stairs to the cellar.

"Run!" Alex screamed, and he bolted right through *The Crazy Clue Course Challenge*. He was long gone by the time a clone grabbed Manfred by his tail. So he didn't know that four others grabbed his friend's legs. And he had no idea that the clones then hoisted the howling dog into the air and carried him through the maze of sets that speckled Cypress Vine's twisted television studio.

Alex hid on the set of a show called *The Guess-ing Game* and prayed that none of the clones had seen him. After a few seconds he knew he was safe—for the moment.

"I hope Manfred's all right," he thought as he pushed a curtain aside and peered out into Cypress's game show factory. He was stuck. If he abandoned his hiding place, he'd be spotted in a split second, no doubt about it. He was going to have to wait until the workday was over, when everything shut down for the night—assuming the evil game show factory ever shut down at all.

A siren blared through the Great House. The

clones stopped what they were doing. The camera operators shut down their cameras. Alex could tell because the red lights on top of each camera switched off. The phony contestants slipped out of their human disguises, the show hosts put down their microphones, and every single clone on that soundstage marched off. Alex tried to see where they were going, but there were too many sets obstructing his view.

Once he thought the final stragglers had passed, Alex stepped out from his hiding space.

"Manfred?" he whispered as loudly as he felt he could without being discovered. "Manfred, where are you?" But there was no answer. "This place is the size of a mall," Alex thought. "It could take me forever to find that dog." He started looking around.

Alex passed through two sets, grabbed a Tootsie Roll from a catering table, and started snooping around another set. And as he peeked around the host's podium to see if Manfred was crouched underneath it, something caught his eye. Alex walked straight toward one of the monitor-covered walls.

"Dad?"

He placed a hand on the TV screen in front of him and pushed on the glass monitor, trying to reach through it. He wanted to touch the man on the other side, or at least get his attention. But his father just sat there with a blank stare on his face.

"Come on, Dad," Alex finally whispered. He tapped on the screen, but his father didn't blink. "Dad!" Alex pounded on the screen. "Dad!" Still nothing. His father wasn't watching Alex. He was watching some prerecorded game show, and he had no idea that his son was watching him watch it.

"Yoo-hoo!" Cypress's nasty voice rang through the Great House's speakers. "Alex, honey, come out, come out, wherever you are." Alex's spine stiffened, and he stood straight up. Somehow, even before he heard Manfred's howls, Alex knew that his friend was in trouble.

"Here's the deal, sweetie." Cypress's patronizing tones were becoming unbearable to Alex. "Your furry little friend here is about to join the family—my family. I thought you should know, just in case you wanted to say good-bye to your pooch."

Alex looked into his dad's blank eyes. "Don't

move," he whispered, and ran off to the far end of the studio, which turned out to be about the distance of three football fields.

Just short of the end, Alex stopped. A row of cameras separated him from Cypress's sea of clones, who had their backs to Alex. They faced a small raised platform. Alex perched behind the cameras to get a close-up.

The original Cypress Vine was standing on the stage. Alex could tell by the scarlet accents in her green dress and by her height—she was at least a foot taller than the others. An enormous crooked smile danced on her face. "That's the other difference between her and all the others," Alex realized. "The clones never smile."

A scary contraption sat beside Cypress. It looked like a compactor that crushes automobiles between two solid metal walls. Only Cypress's compactor did not have flat walls. Half of a mold had been sculpted into each side. The mold on the left was of the left side of Cypress's body. Her left arm, her left leg, her left stomach, her left head, her left side. The mold on the right was of her body's right side. And both halves together made one Cypress Vine. Between the two halves of the compactor's molded walls, tied to a stake, waiting to be pressed into a Cypress Vine clone, sat Manfred, howling desperately.

"We're just waiting for our guest of honor," Cypress explained to her audience, "and then we'll begin. Alex, darling," she called, "whenever you're ready."

Cypress would have been incredibly disappointed if she'd known that Alex, perched behind the row of TV cameras, was not shaking with fear. He was not crying, he was not nauseated, he was not wavering, and most importantly, he was not feeling defeated. He was, in fact, developing a plan.

"If you come out," Cypress chirped sweetly, "I'll give you a cookie." She held up the final fortune cookie. "Honestly. Come up here, and it's yours."

"Deal!" Alex screamed. He didn't believe Cypress's promise, but he now had his plan. The army of clones turned. Under their menacing glares Alex held his ground and looked right through the clones. He winked at Manfred, who tried to smile but couldn't quite manage it.

"Let him through," Cypress instructed her subordinates. The clones parted without a word, and Alex walked up to the stage.

"Well?" he said, and he stuck his hand out, palm up.

Cypress dropped the cookie into his hand. "It won't do you any good." She laughed. "Your last fortune was bogus. The End isn't in here."

Alex shrugged. "Sort of puts a damper on your plans, doesn't it?" he asked. "I mean, even if you do manage to hypnotize the rest of my world, what good will it do you if you can't get in yourself? So much for your slave race of game show junkies."

"Don't worry about me, A, I'll find another way. Besides, it's poor form to mix business and pleasure. Let's talk about my domination of your pathetic species after we induct the two new members of the family."

"Two?" Alex asked.

"You're next, sweetie." Cypress smiled. She pressed a button on the side of her ominous contraption. The two molded walls began to close in on Manfred. He howled for his life. As the walls moved closer and closer, Cypress laughed harder and harder. So Alex joined her.

"What are you laughing at?" Cypress demanded.

"This." Alex smiled, and he shoved the unopened fortune cookie between the compressing walls before they met and molded his friend. The machine's gears started to grind. They couldn't break the cookie. Alex knew there was nothing in the entire universe that could break that cookie before it reached its End. The grinding grew louder and louder. The gears began to smoke as a burning smell filled Alex's nose. The gearbox burst into flames. Gaskets, bolts, pistons, rods, and all sorts of other parts popped out of the machine and whizzed across the room.

The entire contraption started shaking and spluttering. In seconds, the two molded walls burst apart and crashed to the floor. They landed with such awesome force that they broke through the stage. Safe at last, Manfred smiled.

Alex bent over, picked up the cookie, and slid it into his pocket.

"You really shouldn't have done that." Cypress grabbed Alex by his ear. Before she could lock her pinch down, he wiggled free and danced over to Manfred.

"I've been thinking, Cypress," Alex taunted as he untied his friend, "and your plan for global domination is pretty ridiculous. I mean, even if you could find a way into my world," he goaded Cypress on, "people are way too smart to fall for your lies. They'll see right through you."

"Really?" Cypress snorted. "Well, let me point something out to you, kid. Look around!" She gestured with her arms raised slightly above her head. Alex and Manfred looked up at the millions of people glued to the TV screens that covered the walls and ceiling of Cypress's lair. "Sloths! The whole lot of 'em. Brainless machines waiting for a master. Numb to the whole world, ready to serve me."

"Of course," Alex argued, "you caught them at their worst moments. When they were low and needed a taste of good luck and positive fortune, you gave them phony game shows and made them believe they had a chance. Just like you did to my dad when my mom died. Just like you're doing to him right now! It's a cheap trick, Cypress."

"So what if it is?" Cypress screeched. "I'm just giving him what he wants. He wants to see schlubs like him chance it all and win big? Fine. I'm happy to provide, because when I give him what he wants, he gives me what I want. Ownership over his will. At first he couldn't shut off his TV, then he couldn't get out of his chair, and now he can hardly move or make a decision or remember to eat. He's just like the rest of them, A. The living dead. They'll do whatever I want, because I'm their host and they're just a bunch of pathetic knuckleheads who can't even tie their own shoes without me!"

DING!

Alex, Manfred, Cypress, and the sea of clones all turned to the sign. As the 9 in 2,748,319 flipped over and became an 8, there was a deafening CRASH! A TV plummeted from the ceiling and smashed to pieces all over the stage.

In the distance, there was another, fainter CRASH! Then another one, closer. Then farther away. Then a whole chorus of them. Each and every one of them was preceded by a DING! And with every television that fell from the ceiling or off a wall, the Great House shrank a little. The more the monitors CRASHED!

and SMASHED!

and EXPLODED!

the smaller the Great House became.

"What is going on?" Cypress seethed. Throughout her TV studio, brainwashed victims reached forward and turned off their televisions. "You!" Cypress picked up Alex by his shirt and held him to her face. "What did you do?"

"Who, me?" Alex giggled. "All I did was hit a few buttons on those big camera thingies over there. Was that bad?"

Cypress dropped Alex. She looked over at the row of cameras Alex had been hiding behind. On top of each camera was a little red light shining brightly, illuminating one tiny word: LIVE. Thanks to Alex, everything Cypress Vine was saying was being broadcast live over her very own Game Show Station.

"Smile, Cypress," Alex said, picking himself up off the ground, "you're on the air. You just personally explained everything to your loyal slaves."

So many people were turning off their TVs now that there was just one long DING! echoing through the room. The giant red number on the board was rapidly spiraling toward a giant red zero. Entire rows of televisions were falling from the walls, and the house was deflating. "Like a Hoodoo after its job is done," Alex thought.

As the studio continued to shrink, one of its massive walls moved toward Alex, Manfred, and the Cypresses. Alex looked up at it just in time to see his dad yawn, smile, and hit the Power button on his remote control. The moment Mr. G. flipped off his TV, the corresponding screen popped off the studio wall and fell to the ground.

The Great House was shrinking so quickly now that its walls smashed into the game show sets. There was simply not enough room for everything anymore. Something was going to have to give. The Deal Wheel ripped right through one side of the house, and the Puzzle Pyramid tore a gaping hole in another. The little that was left of the place shook, rattled, and quaked until finally the structure gave and the walls of the Great House crashed down to the ground.

chapter

16

Alex, Manfred, and Cypress Vine stood on top of Kismet Mountain, amid an army of clones and a pile of rubble that had once been Cypress Vine's kingdom. Lying by a puddle that had once been a moat, Alex saw a shattered television set. The woman on it was giving her head a good shake. She stretched out her arms, cracked her neck, and reached toward the screen. Then the beat-up TV went blank. A muffled DING! rose from one of the piles of debris, and the once boastful sign flipped to zero.

The incredible sounds of destruction rang up and down Kismet Mountain, and its many residents hurried to see what all the noise was about. Imagine their surprise when they saw a thousand Cypress Vines standing on a pile of trash.

The creatures of Kismet Mountain pushed forward, standing face-to-face with the clones. Everywhere they looked, they saw the face of the woman who had kidnapped their children so many years ago. Every one of them was overflowing with rage. Including Manfred.

"Witchily woman!" Manfred barked, exhausted and enraged. "Liar!" He grabbed one of the thousand Cypresses by her arms and squeezed her so tightly that she was lifted off the ground. "You promised us that if we did what you wanted, our children would be safe! So where are they?"

The clone wriggled in Manfred's arms.

"Oh, nopes! Where do you think you're going?" Manfred squeezed even harder. "Tell us where our children are, or you will suffer as much as we have!"

A tear formed in Cypress's eye.

"You want to balliop and cry?" Manfred growled. "I'll give you something to balliop about." And he squeezed her so hard that she split right down the center.

Shocked, Manfred dropped her. He took a step back as the clone hit the ground and cracked open like an egg. From the Cypress shell emerged the most amazing thing Alex had ever seen. A curly-haired puppy.

"J-J-Junior?" Manfred stammered.

"Pops?" the just-hatched dog asked.

As Manfred embraced his lost pup, Alex could see that the first domino had fallen. And that was all it took. Manfred's six other pups hatched next—four more boys and two girls. Then Cypress's entire army of clones started to crack, freeing all the children of Kismet Mountain.

Alex smiled at the awesome sight. Parents pushed through the crowd searching for their lost children. To his left, a two-ton whale shed its Cypress skin, like a snake, and spilled out all over the place. His father—the Whale of a Good Time—whooped with joy for the first time in years.

The Great House had fallen, and the children of Kismet Mountain had returned home. With his kids dancing around him, Manfred looked at his friend Alex and smiled, tears running down his furry face. It was a joyous day for everyone—

well, almost everyone. Out of the corner of his eye, Alex noticed Cypress Vine quietly slinking away.

"Hey!" Alex hollered so loudly that everyone on top of that mountain turned toward him. "Where do you think you're going, Cypress?"

"Oh, um, I was just, uh, you know, hon, I have a . . . dentist appointment and I can't be late."

"I don't think so, hon," Alex shot back. The creatures of Kismet Mountain surrounded Cypress Vine, making escape impossible. "Don't you have anything to say to all these people?"

"Uh, sorry?" Cypress tried.

"Say it like you mean it," Alex insisted.

Cypress tried again. "So sorry." It was even more pathetic than her first attempt. The crowd inched in closer, looking as if it wanted to tear the witch's head off.

"You can't, can you?" Alex asked.

"Nope." Cypress shook her head and smiled awkwardly.

"She can't say it like she means it, because she doesn't mean it," Alex explained to the crowd. "She doesn't even know she's done anything wrong." And then he added, "Yet."

Alex stared into Cypress's solid black eyes. "What are you looking at?" Cypress demanded.

"Popper?" Alex spoke to Cypress's left eye, hoping that his frumpy little friend with the eyeball for a head would hear him. "Popper, you in there?"

Cypress's left eye winked.

"Get down to the Hoodoo, Popper. You have to tell Zipper to start pumping! That's the only way Cypress will ever understand all this." Alex pointed at the crowd of people standing ankle-deep in the remains of the Great House and discarded Cypress shells. "Do it!" Alex screamed into Cypress's eye. "Now!"

Alex stepped away from Cypress. Everyone on top of that mountain, including Cypress (but not Manfred), looked at him as though he were a nut. They, of course, knew nothing about Popper, Zipper, or Cypress's defective Hoodoo.

"Hey, Pops," one of Manfred's daughters asked, "is your friend, you nose, all right up-stairs?"

"Just give wee-Popper a minuet," Manfred said.

And that was all it took. A minute later Cypress

suddenly gripped her stomach with both hands and moaned, "Oh my!" She was in agony. "My aching belly! Oh!" She looked around at the creatures of Kismet Mountain, at the ruins of her Great House, at the smashed-in television screens, at the splintered game show sets, and at Alex. A tear formed in her eye. She fell to the ground and balled up in pain. Then a flood of tears poured from her eyes and washed the solid black away.

Cypress convulsed on the ground. Her abdomen began to inflate like a balloon. The creatures of Kismet Mountain watched in amazement as the witch continued to expand. And no one was more surprised than Cypress when, a moment later, she was lifted off the ground.

"Stop her!" Manfred's oldest son barked as Cypress began to float away. But it was too late.

Up she went—straight into the sky and out of sight. Above the noise of the murmuring crowd, Alex could have sworn he heard Cypress squeak, "I'm sorry," just before she disappeared from sight.

With Cypress gone and their children back, the creatures of Kismet Mountain decided there was really only one thing they could do. "Party!" the Whale of a Good Time shouted, and he led his friends back down the mountain to celebrate.

"You coming?" Manfred asked Alex.

"Nah." Alex shook his head. "I'd like to, but I think that's for me." He smiled, pointing over Manfred's shoulder at a freshly painted red door with a sparkling gold knob that had appeared in the middle of the rubble.

"You nose," Manfred laughed, "I was–am thinking that I'll send that old ele-fant a present."

"What elephant?" Alex asked.

"The shoe salesman-ing ex-guru. The one who told me that you'd show up here one day. Yes, I mustard send him a fruitcake."

"Elephants eat fruitcakes?" Alex asked.

"Allpeoples eat fruitcakes," Manfred explained.

Manfred shook his curly gray-and-white head and gave Alex a big furry hug. "It was an honor to nose you, Alexgrindlay." Manfred smiled. "You're one lucky gun of a son."

Alex gave Manfred a good scratch behind the ears, and that was that.

He walked over to the red door and tried the knob. The door was locked. He looked down at his feet. Written on the straw doormat he was standing on were two words: THE END. Alex pulled the final fortune cookie out of his pocket, looked back at Manfred and his family, and waved good-bye.

When he split the cookie in half, the red door creaked open. Alex stepped inside, and the door closed behind him.

Though one journey ends, another begins.

Alex stepped out onto Geisel Lane, and the rusted-out gate closed behind him. He turned back. The Cookie Company was gone. Sitting in its place was a small gold sign nailed to a stick that was stuck in the ground. Black stenciled letters read:

1228 GEISEL LANE
FOR LEASE

The sun reflected off the small sign, and Alex decided it was a beautiful morning to take a walk.

As he walked up his driveway, he saw that his

father's bedroom window was smashed—most likely by the shattered TV that was lying on the front lawn, Alex guessed. He walked inside and stumbled upon a most unexpected scene. His father was downstairs in the kitchen, cooking breakfast.

"Hey, Alex!" His dad smiled. "I thought you left for school already."

"Oh," Alex explained, "I, um, forgot my homework."

"I'm glad you did, 'cause look at me"—his dad laughed—"I'm cooking!"

"I see that." Alex giggled. "But why . . ."

"I don't know." Mr. G. flipped a pancake into the air and caught it in his pan. "I guess there was nothing to watch on TV. Besides, there's so much I want to do today, I thought I'd better get an early start."

By nine that morning, Alex Grindlay had already managed to shower, dress, put in both contact lenses, sneeze before flossing (avoiding sending any dental floss into his head and out his left nostril), hop over the broken step second closest to the bottom of the staircase without inci-

180

dent, grab his homework, wolf down some of his father's homemade breakfast, wander into the boys' (as opposed to the girls') bathroom, and slide safely into his desk a full minute before Ms. Figelman began taking roll call.

He turned around and faced the exquisitely braided Sarah Sachs. She looked down at his feet, at his white sneakers. Her silver-covered teeth sparkled when she smiled.

"What are you doing this afternoon?" Alex asked.

"Nothing. Why?"

"Because it turns out there was a cure for my Hoodooitis after all. A bet's a bet. I owe you a piece of pizza and a Coke."

Sarah giggled. "I thought you'd never ask."

Ms. Figelman began taking attendance. Alex turned forward and unzipped the front pocket of his knapsack. Sitting among his many pens and pencils was a single fortune cookie. As he picked it up, he heard a burping pigeon of a car horn outside. Alex looked out the window just in time to see Sal's five-wheeled Express Delivery truck rounding the corner.

Alex examined the cookie in his hand. He took

a deep breath. "Oh well, what's the worst that can happen?" he asked himself. And then he broke the cookie in two.

He pulled out the fortune to see what it had to say. But there was nothing written on it. He flipped it over. There was nothing there, either. It was blank, completely blank.

He smiled and reached for a pen.

About the Author

Ross Venokur has had several jobs in his life, including:

Hot-air balloon blower
Llama roper
Macaroni-and-cheese reviewer
Moon catcher
Rainbow suspender tester
Banjo picker
Sand and dirt organizer
Pixie chaser
Superhero trainer
Grass grazer
and
Horseradish sculptor.

Of all his many occupations, he likes being a writer the best.